I0831913

Into the Abyss

Scourge of Scotland

Marissa Price

The Literature Factory
Publishing Division
Hudson Way, Ningi
Queensland, Australia 4511

www.theliteraturefactory.com.au

Published by The Literature Factory, 2018

A catalogue record for this book is available at the State Library of Queensland

Paperback ISBN 978-0-6481279-2-5
eBook ISBN 978-0-6481279-3-2
Hardcover ISBN 978-0-6481279-5-6

Printed by IngramSpark

For Marie and Mary
For your patient teaching of how to speak with a Scottish accent

Into the Abyss

Scourge of Scotland

Chapter One

"Harriet!" Carolyn Hunter's excited voice floated through their rented log cabin. The front door slammed shut, barring the bitter cold and flurries of snow from entering the house.

"Hmmm?" Harriet replied from her cosy position next to the fireplace. She looked up from her tablet and the Google pages she had been researching. She hastily closed an email that she had been toying with…she had never actually intended to send it.

"Look what I found!" Carolyn beamed at her daughter, waving what looked like a discoloured sheet of paper in her hand. Harriet stood up and padded over to her mother, her slippers slapping on the polished wooden floorboards of the little cottage. She grabbed an apple from the bowl on the table as she passed, taking a big bite of the fresh, glossy red fruit.

"It looks just like you!" Carolyn beamed at Harriet, her face alight. She turned the page around and showed Harriet an image of her own face, one that was terribly familiar. Harriet's apple bounced onto the floor as she lost her grip on the snack. Her jaw went slack with disbelief. Carolyn bent down to pick up the apple and handed it back to her daughter. Sitting down heavily on the stool tucked underneath the kitchen bench, Harriet took the paper from her clearly delighted mother.

"I found it in a little bookshop down the street!" Carolyn exclaimed. "I was browsing through the shelves and I saw this ancient book tucked into the encyclopaedia section. When I picked it up, this fell out." It was clear that the parchment had been folded many times over. It was heavily creased, but Carolyn had smoothed it out considerably on her trip back to the cabin. Her father and brothers had not yet returned: presumably they'd decided to do something else once they had headed into the little town just a few minutes' walk from the cottage.

Harriet pondered how to respond as her mind raced. The picture was familiar to her because she had drawn it herself. But the story of how it had come to be was complicated, and her mother would think she was mad if she tried to explain.

"Well? Doesn't it look the spitting image of you?" Carolyn demanded, her face tipping to look at her daughter more closely. Her eyes narrowed suspiciously as she noticed that Harriet's face was a little white, and she realised that her daughter hadn't yet responded.

"Ah," Harriet stalled for time as her thoughts spun uselessly. "Ah, yeah. It does look like me, I guess. Weird huh." She fell back on her old trick of saying nothing. Her mother often said having a conversation with her could be like drawing blood from a stone.

Carolyn held the drawing up to the light. "I wonder how old it is? It looks like an antique. The little old lady at the shop just let me have it! She said she had no use for it, and when I showed her a photo of you on my phone she said that I must give it to you. I suppose she saw the resemblance too." Carolyn put the drawing down on the bench and went to the fridge. She took out the water jug and offered her daughter a drink by raising one eyebrow. Harriet nodded, and her mother retrieved two glasses from the tall cupboard beside the oven. "Found them first time!" Carolyn crowed. The Hunter family had only arrived in the quaint little cottage a few days ago, perched as it was just outside the historical town of Richmond in Tasmania. They were staying in the little getaway lodge near Hobart for the winter solstice for what was their first holiday in quite a long time. Carolyn's work had kept her relentlessly occupied for the last few years and there hadn't been any time for family trips. But this year, Carolyn had managed to finagle a week away from her job as a hot shot lawyer, which was just enough time to take part in the Winter Feast and festivals of Hobart, held over the shortest days of the year.

Harriet smirked as she thought about the activity they had planned for the next day. The crown jewel in their family trip. The Winter Solstice Nude Swim was something her brothers had always wanted to do. Plunging into sub zero temperature waters in nothing more than her birthday suit did not appeal to Harriet at all. But Mason and Tristan had been champing at the bit to participate in the annual, all ages run since they had first heard about it as small children, and so here they were, a day out from the famous Tasmanian activity. There was no way Harriet was getting into the water, but she couldn't wait to see her brothers freeze their butts off. The main swim was tomorrow morning, but since everyone of all ages would be running nude, they were heading down at dusk so the boys could still do the iconic plunge without an audience. And so that Carolyn and Logan wouldn't need to explain the birds and the bees to the boys.

Carolyn set Harriet's glass of water in front of her. "Have you been on that thing all afternoon, Harry?" she asked, wrinkling her nose. "What ARE you researching, anyway? You could have come with me, you know. The bookstore in Richmond is lovely, you would adore it."

"I didn't know they had a bookstore, actually," Harriet mused. She loved reading, but there was a reason she had been avoiding going into the town centre with her family since they had been in Richmond. On their trip through Richmond's main street to get to their cabin, Logan Hunter, Harriet's father, had pointed out the original architecture of the town. The imposing church spires and the elegance of the Richmond Bridge had awed her, but they had also been an uncomfortable reminder of her experience last summer that she knew she couldn't tell her family about.

"You should come with me tomorrow, before we go down to Hobart for the festival," Carolyn said brightly. "To be honest, I hope your brothers don't catch their death running in that freezing river water. But you never know. If you go in, perhaps that colour will wash out of your hair." Carolyn smirked good naturedly.

"They're pretty invincible," Harriet replied, amusement flirting with the corners of her mouth. "Annoying, but pretty indestructible." She smiled cheekily and ignored the barb about her slightly more fiery hair colour. Carolyn threw her an amused look, but she said nothing.

"Where are Dad and the boys?" Harriet asked.

"Oh they got distracted exploring the old Church," Carolyn said, turning away from the counter and taking off her outside coat. Little flurries of snow that had not yet melted drifted down to the floor, beginning to puddle as soon as they touched solid ground.

"Darn," Carolyn said, trying to bunch her jacket up to stop the leaking. "I always forget to take this off at the door." She grabbed the dish cloth and began to wipe up the water on the floor, holding her jacket over her head. Eventually she tossed it in the vicinity of the front door.

"I'm a little chilly," Carolyn said, folding the cloth over the top of the faucet. "I think I might have a shower before Dad and the boys get back. I won't be long." Carolyn slipped out of the kitchen and headed to the spiral staircase leading to the top floor of the cabin.

As soon as Harriet judged her mother was at the top and out of hearing, she pounced. She snatched at the paper her mother had found, crumpling the corner of it slightly as she gripped it tightly.

There was no doubt that this drawing was hers. She had created it a few months ago, when she'd been studying Shakespeare's Romeo and Juliet in English class.

Harriet sat studying the face on the paper, a spitting image of her own eyes, nose and mouth framed by a cloud of shimmering brown hair, unrestrained and tumbling down over her shoulders. It was an image of what Harriet had looked like two months ago, anyway.

Harriet's brain swirled in a kaleidoscope of memories from 14th Century Verona, and her trip back into Juliet's life after she had been rudely ripped from her own. Harriet was still searching for the key to how she had been catapulted back in time, but it seemed that no matter how hard she looked, the wonders of the internet had little to offer except for conspiracy theories and outlandish stories of people who claimed they had travelled through time.

A little like me, I suppose, Harriet mused, turning the paper over in her hands. Why had this surfaced now? What were the odds of her mother finding this tucked into an old book in an obscure bookshop in a small Tasmanian town? Which book had it come from? Would it tell her anything she didn't already know? Questions slammed through Harriet's mind, each one more feverish than the last, until they crossed over each other again and again. Her mother had been right, the parchment looked old. It certainly wasn't the white copy paper she had originally sketched the drawing onto – it looked like it had travelled the 400 years back to their present time the long way, unlike Harriet's instant return. Yet, the paper looked well-loved and despite its age, well cared for. It had the air of a treasured possession. Harriet felt the connection with the drawing, wondered at it – was this the answer to how she could travel through time rifts? It certainly seemed as though this piece of paper had taken her back in time, to the lives of Juliet Capulet and Romeo Montague, to blood feuds and love matches in the time of arranged marriages. And equally importantly, it had presumably returned her to her own time. That was the reason why she hadn't let the drawing out of her sight in Verona – she hadn't wanted to risk her ticket home. But something nagged at Harriet's memory, much like it had since she had returned to Tasmania in the 21st Century. There was something missing.

Harriet drummed her fingers on the bench as she considered what to do. The compulsion to keep the parchment safe was as strong as it had been in Verona. She could take the drawing and hide it, hoping her mother would forget about it in the rush of her father and brothers arriving back at the cabin. Or she could play it cool and pretend it was no big deal: just a drawing that happened to look a little bit like her. Which would be more believable? What if she took it and her mother demanded that she show it to the rest of the family?

Harriet considered her options. She was a teenager – she could definitely pull off bored and uninterested.

The piping voices of her brothers floating over the soft shush of falling snow, and the lower, deeper rumbling of her father's voice carrying to the cabin forced Harriet's hand and made her panic. She judged that she had about 15 seconds before the rest of her family descended on the kitchen. She swiped the drawing off the counter and took it with her over to her armchair near the fire place, picking up her tablet as she plopped down into the seat again. She heard the shower shut off and knew that it wouldn't be long before her mother joined them again, too. Tossing the drawing onto the coffee table in front of her, Harriet tucked her legs back underneath her body and sank into the chair, affecting an air of contentment and relaxation.

On cue, Logan, Mason and Tristan came inside in a blast of cold air. The boys went to run towards the warmth of the inner cabin, but they were seized by the back of the jackets.

"No you don't," Logan Hunter said mildly, effortlessly holding each of his sons slightly off the ground. Their legs peddled ineffectively through the air, the grins on their faces gleaming in the cabin's soft light.

"Jackets off first, then straight into the shower for the pair of you," Logan said, his tone soft and patient, but not to be trifled with. Logan's children did not tangle with him. Mason and Tristan instinctively obeyed the command in their father's tone, and as he set them back down on their feet, they began to strip off their jackets.

Carolyn came down the spiral staircase as her sons reached the bottom of it, dancing on the spot as they waited for their mother to descend. It was a tiny staircase, and only one person could go up or down it at any one time.

Carolyn ruffled each of her sons' hair as they bounded past her and up towards their room. Logan came further into the cabin and gave his wife a kiss before smiling warmly at Harriet.

"Have a good time with your tech thingy?" Logan asked his daughter with a twinkle in his eye. Harriet shrugged, but a grin snuck onto her face. It was hard to not be happy when her father was around, and his lack of ability to understand or use technology was endearing.

"Oh Logan, you have to see what I found today!" Carolyn exclaimed, hurrying to the kitchen counter. She turned to look at Harriet when she realised the drawing was gone, a question on her lips.

"It's there," Harriet headed her off, trying for a faintly bored tone.

Carolyn strode over to pick up the drawing from the coffee table. Logan shivered a little as he waited patiently.

"It looks exactly like Harriet!" Carolyn said, turning the drawing over to show her husband. He took a long look.

"It really does," he agreed, looking from the drawing to his daughter. Harriet held on tightly to her bored indifference. "Would you look at that," he murmured. "Where did you find it, Caro?"

"In the little bookshop in Richmond, just after you left with the boys to look at the old Church. It was tucked into this old book and it fell out when I lifted it up. So did an awful lot of dust," Carolyn said, wrinkling her nose. "I don't think it's been moved in quite a while. Or cleaned."

Harriet restrained herself. She really wanted to know which book her mother had found the drawing in, but she didn't want to give away how important the answer could be to her. She forced herself to remain silent and seemingly engrossed in her screen.

"You're shivering, Logan," Carolyn said, poking at her husband's arm. "Go and get into a warm shower too, before you catch a cold. I'll start dinner."

"Are you sure?" Logan asked. He couldn't entirely suppress the concern that crept into his tone. Carolyn laughed.

"It'll be fine, worrywart!" she said. "Harriet will help me, won't you Harry?" Carolyn turned to her daughter. Harriet put her tablet down and affected an exaggerated sigh.

"I'll make sure she doesn't burn the house down, or cut any fingers off," Harriet said in a mischievous tone. Carolyn aimed a half-hearted smack at her daughter as she sauntered past, but a chuckle escaped from her. She was under no illusions that cooking wasn't one of her strengths. Logan chuckled as he took the spiral staircase two steps at a time.

Harriet had been making fun, but Logan's concern was justified.

"So…scrambled eggs and soup?" Carolyn suggested. "I feel like something warm. And relatively easy." Carolyn winked.

"Sure," Harriet said, whisking the tea towel from its holder. "But I'm in charge, Mum."

Carolyn held up her hands in a gesture of surrender. She grinned. "How can I help, Boss?"

Chapter Two

Harriet had managed to avoid any more questions about the drawing over dinner, through cleaning up, the saga that was the brushing of teeth and the boys' bedtime stories. Carolyn had been distracted with her sons, and before that with wiping up the fallout from her charcoaled toast. Her cooking efforts had set off the fire alarm, but luckily they had a resident fireman to fix the situation. Logan had chuckled at his wife as she sat down to dinner, flustered and with a smear of blackened butter across her cheek.

Harriet was now tucked up in her bed, a low trundle made up in front of the fireplace. She preferred it that way, even though it was a little isolated. She didn't have to share with her brothers in their bunk beds and she was on an entirely different floor of the house to the rest of her family. It made her feel a little more independent. She was nearly 16 after all, and halfway through Year 10. In just a few months she would decide which senior subjects she would do and whether she would sit the TCE exams in Year 12. Harriet had no idea what she actually wanted to do with her life – or what she would need to do to get there – but her school had been holding seminars and her mother had been attempting to have conversations about her future. Harriet knew that Carolyn wanted her to do Legal Studies, but she also knew her mother was trying to hold back from doing anything that might guide Harriet into the life she had chosen for herself. It wasn't anything that her mother had said, per se, Harriet could just sense the caution her mother used when broaching the subject with her.

Harriet stared into the flickering flames of the fire and remembered another time, not that long ago, when she had stared into a fire just like this one. Certainly she hadn't been as comfortable, tucked under her feather doona as she was, and the weather had been much milder than the brutally freezing temperatures of a Tasmanian winter. But she remembered the details of that night well.

Juliet Capulet. One half of history's most infamously doomed lovers. That night by the fire, that conversation, was the first time that the two young women had really connected as individuals, even though they had both been able to feel the invisible connection between them the moment they had met.

Harriet shifted in her blankets and rolled fully onto her side, tucking her hands under her head. It was strange to think that Juliet had been a better friend to her than the girls in her own time. As had Caterina. She often thought about what it would be like to have them here, in her own time. They would certainly be much better company than the girls she went to school with.

Gracie Finkle had always been a thorn in her side. Since they had been in kindergarten, Gracie had delighted in embarrassing Harriet, leaving her out of games and spreading rumours about her. For years Harriet had shrugged it off, but her most recent play had been particularly vicious and cold hearted. Gracie's latest stunt was a large part of why her mother left her new hair colour largely alone. Although Carolyn and Logan didn't think Harriet knew, she was also aware that her problems at school were mostly behind the reason for this mid-year holiday. The boys wanting a dip in the Derwent just worked out well.

Harriet's best friend, Tessa, has always been by her side. They had weathered primary school, the transition to high school and the taunting of the mean girls together. But Tessa had always wanted to be one of the cool kids: one of the girls who was someone. No matter how badly they had treated her in the past. Unfortunately for Harriet, Tessa's recent invitation into the cool crowd came with one big condition…she could no longer be friends with Harriet. When they walked around in their big clique at school, Harriet noticed that Tessa didn't yet have the stomach to actively participate when Gracie taunted her, but neither did she stop the attacks on Harriet. She would look at her shoes, shifting uncomfortably from side to side until Gracie moved on to someone else. But Tessa had no problem walking past Harriet as if she'd never met her, never stayed up until all hours of the night texting and giggling, never shared secrets with each other that they'd never tell anyone else.

A large part of Harriet grieved for the friendship she'd had with Tessa. She didn't make friends with girls easily – they were usually far too much work for her liking – and she missed the time that they spent together. Todd, Tessa's boyfriend, had upgraded into the popular crowd alongside Tessa, of course. Their little trio was no longer, and Harriet was on her own.

But there was still Gideon.

Despite the teasing and taunting from the other kids, Gideon did what he wanted. He could afford to, as he was effortlessly popular on his own without needing the approval of the ruthless kids, the ones who built their popularity on top of the people they stepped all over. Gideon had intervened in Gracie's attacks on Harriet more than once, and she was grateful for it. Unfortunately, his involvement had also intensified the rumours that they were a couple, but Gideon didn't seem to care. He just shrugged it off, and sometimes even came to sit with her at lunchtimes as if in direct defiance of what anyone else might say. Gideon had been in the same classes as both Harriet and Gracie since kindergarten and so he was well aware of what he was dealing with. He was also incredibly handsome, and so lots of the girls fell over themselves trying to get closer to him. Harriet didn't, of course. She had far more dignity than that.

But maybe I do like him, just a little, Harriet mused, mesmerised by the dancing flames. When she allowed her mind to wander without considering the pros and cons of everything, as it usually did, it arrived at a more honest interpretation of what she felt.

He's really quite gorgeous, she smiled a little to herself. She twisted a lock of her shimmering, deep red hair around her finger as she thought. Gideon White certainly was attractive. So good looking, in fact, that Gracie had made a fool of herself several times in the years they had all been thrown together. Harriet gained a certain satisfaction from knowing that Gideon's indifference to Gracie infuriated her. Gracie had tried on numerous occasions to cosy up to Gideon, to flirt and toss her hair at him, but he was consistently unmoved by her efforts.

And maybe that makes him even more appealing, Harriet grinned. But she sobered quickly. Harriet was miserable at flirting, and was only just starting to notice the boys instead of being irritated by them. She had thought that sending Gideon an email might have been easier than talking to him, but she couldn't think of anything to say. Harriet had spent most of her afternoon alone in the cottage trying to put something witty and clever into a draft email while she flicked between search browsers for information on time travel. But it wasn't to be, and she had checked that any attempts at reaching out to Gideon had been well and truly deleted from her account.

Losing Tessa had created a much larger crater in Harriet's life than she had initially expected. Carolyn and Logan had seen the damage developing, even though their daughter had been unable to. They saw this trip as a way of hitting the reset button for Harriet and allowing her some breathing space from her usual environment and routine. And typical of the trials of parenting teenagers, they had done their best to avoid clueing her into that and meeting the brick wall of resistance Harriet was fully capable of building.

Unable to sleep, Harriet reached over to the coffee table and slid her tablet into her hands. Her current research blinked onto the screen as she hit the power button. Everything she had found was there, and it all seemed beyond crazy. No one in their right mind would believe that a 16-year-old from Tasmania had spent a week kicking around in medieval Italy, and not a single person from her own time had noticed.

Brooding, Harriet reflected on how she had felt since her return from Verona. She missed Juliet and Caterina, and the easy relationship they had enjoyed. She felt lonely. Harriet also missed the action and drama, as tense as it had been at times. Harriet had never seen herself as a thrill seeker, but there was something about travelling into a life so different to your own that was pretty exciting. And determining how much of that travel had been real, and how much imaginary, was infuriating her.

For months, Harriet had been researching Romeo and Juliet. The original play written by Shakespeare was still everywhere, not that Harriet had actually re-read it. She'd been too busy looking for real people who might have inspired the characters of Juliet and Caterina. A lot of the information around the play seemed a little different, somehow, from what she remembered reading before she had experienced Juliet's time firsthand. The idea that Shakespeare's works had been largely based on real people was a theory that had been debated for centuries. It seemed to depend on the story. For the life of her, Harriet couldn't recall there being any information on the real people who might have inspired the story of Romeo and Juliet when she had written her English assignment last term. There was now, although the details were sketchy and shady. Harriet didn't know whether this was because she was simply looking for it now, though. In other Shakespearean plays, there were clear links to real people, like Anne in Henry VIII or many of the characters in Julius Caesar. But also woven into those tales were various supernatural phenomena that quite simply didn't exist. At least, not if you were a rational person.

Harriet blew out a frustrated breath. She was back in the mental circle she had travelled for months, not clearly understanding which way to go. Harriet wanted – no, needed – to know how she could travel back in time, and for what purpose. Would it happen to her again? And how? Now that she had the drawing again, could she open another time rift?

Harriet frowned. The drawing didn't seem to be the whole story. She had carried it all through Verona, and despite wishing numerous times to return to her own world, the drawing had not opened a portal. It didn't seem to control the time travel, or at least her use of it didn't.

Eventually, Harriet's eyes drooped as her mind quietened, humming away at a level that became increasingly less intense. Her tablet screen blinked off and slid softly to the side as Harriet shifted silently into her twilight dreams.

Chapter Three

"Harry, wake up!" Mason insisted, his face two inches from his sister's. His small hand shook her shoulder relentlessly. Harriet murmured in her sleep and turned away from her youngest brother.

Mason's exasperated expression set to mulish. But then an evil grin spread over his freckled face. Beckoning to Tristan, who had been watching the exchange, he snuck onto the couch behind Harriet's trundle bed. Tristan, smirking as he saw his little brother's plan, headed around to the other side of Harriet, squeezing in between her and the coffee table. Mason got right up close to Harriet's face, her deep, soft breathing fluttering his eyelashes.

"Boo!" he yelled, cackling as he whipped his head back out of Harriet's reach. Her eyes flew open and she rolled backwards, straight into Tristan's open arms. He wasted no time bundling his sister up in the blankets and holding her down as Mason launched himself from the back of the couch, confident that his sister was pinned down. He began to tickle, mercilessly.

"Stop! Stop….st-st-stop, Mason!" Harriet cried between sleepy gales of laughter. She was extremely ticklish, and her brothers knew it. Thankfully she was so trussed up that neither of them could get at her feet.

"Leave her alone, boys," Logan said mildly from the breakfast table tucked into the sunny nook beside the kitchen. He sipped his coffee. "And don't touch her feet. The last time I did, she kicked me in the face."

Harriet sat up quickly, tucked her feet more deeply into the blankets. Her brothers backed away, cheeky smiles wreathing their faces. They leaped back into their seats at the table beside their father as Carolyn came down the spiral stairs.

Harriet threw back the blankets and padded over to sit with her family. Her father pushed a plate towards her and Harriet began to shovel scrambled eggs laced with bacon into her mouth. She closed her eyes in bliss. Delicious.

"So Harry, I'm going back into town before we leave for the festival this afternoon. I thought I might show you that little bookstore, if you wanted to come with me?" Carolyn took a long sip of her coffee. She smiled in appreciation. Carolyn didn't function very well before her morning caffeine dose.

Harriet jumped on the chance before it disappeared. "Sure, I'll come for a look," she said. Carolyn was mildly surprised, but she hid it well. Her daughter didn't often choose to accompany her to anything these days – she wasn't going to look a gift horse in the mouth.

"Okay then! I thought we might leave in about half an hour," Carolyn said, collecting her sons' plates to take into the kitchen.

"No problem," Harriet said, swallowing the last of her breakfast. "Just let me have a quick shower and we can go." Without being obvious about it, Harriet swiped the drawing her mother had found off the coffee table on her way upstairs, stashing it in her suitcase to deal with later.

***

Harriet and Carolyn stepped out together and locked the door behind them. The boys had already left for a walk through the nearby forest full of skeletal trees, barren branches laden with snow.

Harriet and Carolyn spoke as they walked, about everything and nothing. Harriet was careful with her responses – she didn't want her mother to get onto the topic of Tessa. She really didn't want to talk about it, but she knew that her mother did. Luckily for her, it wasn't long before they hit the outskirts of Richmond's town proper and Harriet became fascinated with the buildings she was walking past. They were newer than they looked, but the whole town was like something out of a postcard.

Carolyn happily explained all that she knew as they walked, and Harriet found herself looking around, wide eyed. The little boutiques and tea shops nestled into Georgian style buildings dating back to the 1800s were fascinating. As they walked, Harriet took in the museums and art galleries, the charming pathways and roads and the little churches dotted throughout the town proper. She deliberately avoided looking at the convict build bridge that reminded her uncomfortably of Italy.

The town wasn't overly large, and before long they stood in front of the shop they were seeking. The tiny bookstore Carolyn had visited the day before was delightful. It had a cute sign hanging over the doorway, swaying slightly in the breeze. The brilliant sunshine of the mid-winter day reflected unrelentingly off the bright white of the snow banks scattered around the façade of the shop. It was picturesque and enchanting, and Harriet was thrilled she was here to enjoy it. Her enchantment grew stronger as they stepped inside the little storefront, the door jingling as they opened it. The gloom relaxed her eyes immediately, but they took a moment to register anything other than hulking shapes after the brilliance of the daylight outside.

Gradually, a room piled with books – books literally everywhere – emerged in her vision. There were new books, old books, small, fat, skinny and tiny books. There were rows and rows of breathtaking, leather bound books. Encyclopaedia sets, their spines glinting gold in the low light, sat on a shelf near the desk where a little old lady sat, knitting a brilliant green scarf.

"Hello, dears," she said, a kindly smile on her face. "Oh! I saw you yesterday, didn't I?" She spoke enthusiastically to Carolyn, who smiled back.

"You did indeed. I've brought my daughter with me to have a look at your store: we couldn't resist coming again. She loves books, and I thought she would enjoy a little look at what you have here."

The lady beamed and spread her arms wide. Despite her multitude of missing teeth, she gave off more of a kind grandma vibe than a scary old lady feeling. "If there's anything I can do to help, just call out." She smiled and went back to her knitting, pulling the stitches through without even seeming to concentrate on her handiwork.

The smell of the store was bewitching. To Harriet, the smell of old books was like ambrosia. The tomes were yellowed with time but full of stories that lay in wait to ensnare and entertain the reader. Carolyn wandered around, her eye caught by a collection of colourful spines. Harriet meandered on her own, looking for a book that fit the description of small, old and dusty that her mother had given. Which wasn't really specific or helpful, given just how many books fit that description in this store.

"Are you looking for something in particular, dear?" The old lady was behind Harriet, giving her a start. She had approached noiselessly: Harriet hadn't even noticed that she had moved. Given the gaps in her teeth, she really should have appeared menacing. But she just didn't.

"Oh I'm fine," Harriet said, trying to sound casual. "Just having a little look."

"Your mother was quite excited to find a drawing yesterday," the old lady mused, resting a gnarled hand on a low table near her hip. "She said that it looked a lot like you, and I must say that she seems to be right. How amazing." The old lady chuckled to herself. As she had been speaking, she had pulled a small, leather bound book out of the collection on the shelf nearest to her. With an enigmatic look for Harriet, she left the book resting on the edge of the shelf and melted back into the shadows she had emerged from.

Harriet acknowledge that she was a little creeped out, despite the little old lady's non-threatening aura.

Moving closer, Harriet studied the book that the lady had left standing out on its own. Picking it up gingerly, Harriet could see it was incredibly old. As she touched the cover she felt a slight tingle, a little like the electric shock that you get sometimes when you touch a shopping trolley or a car door. It stopped after a moment and Harriet turned the book over in her hands. The cover was brown and non-descript, but when she opened it she could see Shakespeare's name scrawled across the first page. The man was everywhere.

The spine was beginning to separate from the pages inside, and it looked a sad sight of a book. The pages were yellowed and the writing was a scrawling script. The ink was severely faded in places, but mostly legible in others. If you could read spider handwriting, that is.

"Oh!" Carolyn said as she came around the corner of a stacked tower of books. "That's the book that I found the drawing in!" She frowned. "You know, it looks so old… it really should be in a museum."

"Hmm perhaps," Harriet said, her spine tingling with suspicion and apprehension. It seemed a little too fated that this book should fall into her hands. After her trip to medieval Italy, Harriet was a bit wary of things that fell into place too easily. And of drawings that looked like her.

"I think we should tell the Richmond Village Museum about it on our way back through," Carolyn said decisively. "It might be historically important."

"I suppose," Harriet said, shrugging and clinging to her non-committal and disinterested act.

Carolyn wandered off to poke around the front window of the store. Harriet felt a little panicked, unsure of what to do. She couldn't afford to let this book get into the hands of the Tasmanian authorities…what if it held the secret to her ability to travel back in time? Anything with Shakespeare's name on it that looked this old would indeed be historically important. Thankfully her mother hadn't seen that part of it. If the museum saw this they would take it, and the secrets that it held would be lost to her forever.

But how was she going to stop that from happening? Harriet glanced around surreptitiously. No-one was watching.

She had always been a good girl, had always done as she was told. What if she took the book into safekeeping, just for the time being. Just until she figured out whether it was the key to her travel, or if it held any other information that she needed to know about this strange new ability she seemed to have.

Not allowing herself to think about it any longer, Harriet slipped the book into the pocket of her coat. She would bring it back when she was finished, she promised herself. It would be like it had never happened.

Harriet shook off a strange feeling of premonition as she and Carolyn left the bookstore and stopped for a hot chocolate in a café before they headed back to the rented cabin. The book felt like it was burning a hole in her pocket as she waited for her mother to order. Or perhaps that was guilt. Glancing around guiltily, Harriet slipped the book from her pocket and flipped through the pages under the table. It seemed as though it was a book of notes, with different headings and characters swimming around together on the pages. One page was titled 'Macbeth', and among the words she recognised, there was one unfamiliar name in bold writing.

Lachlan, Harriet mused. If this was an old book of notes about Shakespeare, perhaps her mother was right and it did belong in a museum. Harriet knew she would have to work hard to distract her mother from detouring to the Richmond Museum on their way back to the cabin. Turning the book over in her hands, she mused that this book looked old enough to have been written by Shakespeare himself.

Harriet looked up blankly, feeling as though she had been struck by lightning. Quickly, and gingerly, she flipped through the pages she was yet to decipher. The headings caught her eye, even though most of the text was a mystery. A Midsummer Night's Dream. Hamlet. Much Ado About Nothing. Harriet recognised them all as titles of Shakespeare's plays. She paged through until she reached the page titled 'Romeo and Juliet'. Squinting, she tried to make out letters and words in the script that was unfamiliar to her, brought up as she had been in the age of Times New

Roman and Arial fonts. Star crossed lovers. Poison. Tragedy. Blood feud.

And there just like the Lachlan scribed onto the Macbeth page, stood another word in bold. Caterina.

Harriet slammed the book shut, her hands shaking. What on earth was going on?

Chapter Four

The sound of her brothers' bickering broke through the old school rock blaring through Harriet's headphones as they headed towards Sandy Beach from Hobart. They had travelled into the city for the end of the Winter Festival and had enjoyed oysters by the water and the sights of the capital. The boys had been snarking at each other all afternoon, but Harriet had barely heard them. She was preoccupied with the thought of the old book sitting cosily in the pocket of her snow jacket.
"Here we are," Logan said, as the tyres of the car scrunched noisily on the frozen gravel littering the side of the road near where the Derwent River Run had taken place that morning. It was sunset and the light was beginning to fade, perfect for a plunge into freezing water when it was only eight degrees outside.
"Definitely be needing these," Carolyn said, pulling piles of blankets, towels and spare clothes out of the boot of the car. She shoved

a load into Logan's arms. Harriet wandered to the back of the car, only to find herself piled high with towels as well.

"I really don't understand why the boys want to do this," Harriet said, her teeth chattering slightly. It was the shortest day of the year, and the cold mist coming off the river was frosty enough without touching the actual water.

"I don't either," Carolyn replied.

"I do," Logan said, a grin on his face. Carolyn sighed and reached for another bag, filled with spare clothes for Logan. "I knew you wouldn't be able to resist, even though you said you weren't interested," Carolyn said, a wry smile on her face. "I packed these just in case." With a quick kiss for his wife, Logan ran to catch up with his sons, whooping with excitement.

"They never really grow out of it," Carolyn said dryly. Harriet grinned at her father's delight.

The Hunter family made their way down to the river, across the crunchy, sandy banks of the river where about a thousand people had plunged into the freezing waters earlier that morning. Harriet laughed to herself: she wouldn't get into those waters, no matter how much she was paid. It was cold enough just standing out on the riverbank. They could see where fires had dotted the beach from earlier that day, their flames warming chilled and mottled skin, and where hundreds of footsteps had churned up the usually tranquil beach.

"I'm just going to grab the camera from the car," Carolyn yelled as she dashed back up the sand. "I need a photo of this!" she chortled back to Harriet.

Harriet perched herself on a rock close to the edge of the water. The Derwent River was a sight to behold, even close to frozen as it was. Its slight waves lapped against the shore in a lulling rhythm that calmed and soothed. The clear water showed the sandy bottom scattered with tiny pebbles. On the horizon, the sun had started to sink and the gloaming of twilight had begun. This close to the Winter Solstice, the remaining sunlight wouldn't last long. Night would soon fall properly.

As Harriet watched her brothers prepare for the plunge into the icy water, she heard the crunch of tyres on the gravel. A silver 4WD pulled up near to where their own car was parked. A bunch of boys about Tristan and Mason's age piled out, following by their parents and what appeared to be an older brother.

Harriet's cheeks coloured as she recognised the build of the young man who had stepped out of the backseat of the car. What on God's green earth was Gideon White doing on the same beach, at the same time? And with her brothers naked! Harriet's face flamed red as she swivelled to see her own family drop their trunks and run into the freezing water.

The White boys swarmed over the beach towards the water. It was really the only way to describe how they descended on the frozen beach. Clearly, they had the same idea as her own brothers. Harriet turned away, embarrassed, as the younger boys stripped down without an ounce of self-consciousness to run in.

Searching for something – anything – to look at, Harriet's gaze collided with Gideon's. He lifted one dark eyebrow and headed across the frozen sand towards her. Harriet, feeling slightly panicked, glanced around for the safety that her mother represented. She remembered the email she had tried to write a million times the day before and her cheeks turned bright red. Harriet saw that Carolyn was rummaging through the boot of their car – she wouldn't be any help at all.

Despite the years that Harriet and Gideon had attended school together, Harriet hadn't yet met the entire White family. She knew his brothers on sight from primary school, as he would hers. Harriet reflected uncomfortably that it seemed almost as though her earlier thoughts of Gideon had conjured him, though she knew that couldn't be true. She definitely hadn't sent that email, had she? Panic clawed at the pit of her stomach as she tried frantically to remember if she had indeed sent that hideous draft to the trash can where it belonged. Harriet watched him approach in stunned horror, crossing every finger and toe that she hadn't accidentally sent something revoltingly embarrassing to the ridiculously good-looking boy standing in front of her.

"Hi," Gideon said, his voice deep and soothing. "I didn't know you were into freezing mid-winter swims as well." Harriet smiled self-consciously, trying desperately to suppress the flaming tinge of her cheeks.

"Oh I'm not," she replied, hugging her arms in an attempt to keep out the cold. "My crazy brothers and father are." She tried hard to sound casual, but her insides were quaking.

"So are mine," Gideon said ruefully. Together they turned and observed their families frolicking in the freezing Derwent.

"Have you never done it then?" Harriet asked.

"Once," Gideon replied with a cheeky smile. "That was enough."

Harriet turned her gaze back to her outrageous family. Tuning into her feelings, she realised that she was acutely aware of Gideon standing beside her. That was new. She focussed on her brothers, trying to block out his addling charisma.

"Look at those stars there," Gideon murmured pointing up into the sky. The stars were just beginning to wink to life, and Harriet saw that he was looking at a cluster of iridescent blue stars she hadn't really noticed before. They sat in a line of three, the top star brighter and more vibrant than its mates.

A squeal of delight from the water brought Harriet's attention back to their siblings. Smiling a little, she watched as her brothers frolicked in the river. But her smile quickly turned to a frown as she looked at Mason. Something seemed wrong, and she moved closer to the edge of the river to see better. Logan and Tristan were out in deeper water, almost to Tristan's chin, facing out towards the middle of the river. Mason was bobbing, but his head was going under every now and again. That was strange. Mason was usually quite a strong swimmer.

"Mason!" Harriet called out, panic creeping into her tone a little. She cupped her hands around her mouth. "Mason, are you okay?"

He didn't respond, but one of his arms went up into the air. Harriet's blood froze. That was the help signal the Hunter family had been taught, the one they all hoped they'd never have to actually use.

"Dad! Tristan!" Harriet screamed, her eyes on Mason's head. Neither turned her way – they couldn't hear her. Harriet spun back towards her mother: she was too far away and couldn't hear her either.

Harriet didn't wait any longer.

She hit the water running, without a thought for the clothes that would weigh her down or the shoes on her feet. Gideon was right behind her.

Mason was about ten metres from the shore, but there appeared to be a drop off where he was trying to stand. Harriet waded desperately through the freezing cold water, her teeth chattering and her lips turning blue. Her heavy winter clothes dragged against the clear river water, her body slowly turning numb as the freezing slush leaked through her layers of clothing to plaster them against her skin. Shivering, she pushed forward, plunging out into the colder, deeper waters of the river.

Harriet reached Mason just as his head went under. She groped for him in the freezing water, ducking her head under to see better as her fingers brushed ineffectively against his frozen skin. She couldn't see a drop off. Resurfacing, freezing water streaming off her hair into the river, Harriet looked around for her brother. And saw him bobbing a few metres away, laughing maniacally. He was swimming alongside Gideon's brother, both grinning at their older siblings who they had tricked into an unplanned swim.

"You couldn't miss out, Harry!" Mason said as he danced out of his sister's reach. A deep chuckle came from Harriet's right. She spun around in the cold water. The mutinous expression on her face wipe the smile right off Gideon's.

"Well…that wasn't a very nice trick," Gideon acknowledged with a grimace. "But you did get to do the Derwent Dip." A smile flirted around the corners of his mouth. Behind his head, Harriet could see the streak of the Milky Way standing in stark contrast to the deepening blue of night, its image reflected on the surface of the river. It would have been breathtakingly beautiful, if it weren't so breathtakingly cold. Harriet shuddered, and she realised that she had lost sensation in her toes.

"Since you're in here anyway…" Gideon said, a wicked smile on his face. His words trailed off as his head dipped under the water. Harriet turned around frantically, striking out towards the shore. A hand wrapped around her ankle and before she knew it, she was drawn back under the frigid water. She struggled and kicked, connecting with something solid.

Harriet sucked in a gigantic breath as her head broke the surface of the river. She turned back to where Gideon had been, a furious expression on her face. His set down would be blistering.

Gideon's head broke the surface clutching his arm in mock pain, his grin still in place. It faded slowly though, as Harriet watched him take in their surroundings with growing alarm. She spun around to see for herself.

Gone were their siblings and families. The sandy beach had disappeared, replaced with what appeared to be a craggy, steep bank looming in the gathering gloom of night time. They could no longer see the bottom of the Derwent, usually visible from the surface of the river. Neither could touch the bottom, and so were treading water in a brackish, almost grey brook. The Milky Way was gone, although the stars were every bit as bright. The bright blue trio pulsed, seeming to taunt Harriet from her spot in the freezing cold water.

Neither had any idea where they were but both knew this wasn't Tasmania. Nothing around them looked familiar anymore: everything had changed.

Chapter Five

"What the…" Harriet exclaimed, her breath coming out in puffs on the cold air as she stared at Gideon, whose dark hair was plastered to his head. Confusion clouded her brain, the blistering set down on the tip of her tongue forgotten.

"What just happened?" Gideon demanded, his face anxious and confused.

Harriet's mind raced and she instinctively swam towards the shore, Gideon prowling in her wake instinctively. She had no words, so didn't even attempt to explain anything as she swam. They struggled out of the still frigid water, using tree roots that were dipping into the river to help them climb the steep bank that hadn't been there when they went under water. It was so cold that their breath showed as puffs of crystals in the night air, and their heavy clothes were waterlogged and intensely cold.

"Are you alright?" Gideon asked, his teeth chattering. He rubbed his arms, attempting to keep the blood circulating.

"Y-y-y-y-e-s-s," Harriet replied, her teeth rattling viciously. "B-b-b-u-t, w-w-h-ere a-are w-w-we?"

"I was going to ask the same thing," Gideon replied. Harriet ruthlessly clamping down on the inclination for her lips to shake. Their clothes were useless, soaked as they were. Night was about to well and truly fall, and tendrils of fog were already starting to wind their way around their feet and ankles.

"This isn't the Derwent," Gideon said. "And I feel strange, like I've lost my stomach on a ride."

"This doesn't even seem like Tasmania," Harriet said, frowning. "Although I feel just as cold."

"Where else could we possibly be?" Gideon asked, a frown furrowing his forehead.

"I have no idea," Harriet said evasively. "I'm just as lost as you are." She felt bad for the white lie – the feeling in the pit of her stomach was familiar. It was the same feeling she had experienced when she had woken in Verona months before.

Harriet drew in a deep breath – she was shivering down to her toes. Her skin was turning blue, and Gideon's wasn't far behind. Then she remembered the old, fragile book in her pocket. Harriet frantically patted at her jacket, relieved to feel the outline of the cover against her fingers. It would be waterlogged by now, but she couldn't do anything about it.

"Wh-what a-are y-y-you l-l-l-looking f-f-f-for?" Gideon asked.

"I h-had a b-b-b-book in my p-p-p-pocket," Harriet replied, her teething clattering against each other.

"Y-y-your w-w-worried about a b-b-b-book right n-n-now?" Gideon finally got the words out. "U-u-unless w-w-we can u-use it to s-s-s-start a f-f-f-fire, d-d-does it m-m-matter?"

Potentially, Harriet mused. Talking was becoming difficult – words didn't want to make it past the chattering of their teeth. She shoved her hands into her pockets, reassured when her fingers brushed against the worn leather of the cover. Harriet yanked it out. It was completely dry.

"W-well, I'll be d-d-damned," Harriet said, her voice breathless from awe and the cold. "It s-s-s-should be c-c-c-c-completely s-s-s-soaked." She turned it over in her hands, marvelling that it was still completely intact. Or at least, it didn't look any older or more dishevelled than when she had pocketed it in the store.

"R-r-right," Gideon said with a swift look at the book. "W-w-warm…n-n-n-now." Harriet simply nodded her agreement – it was too tiring to attempt to speak.

The pair started away from the river, walking back up the bank. Far ahead of them they could see a dark outline that appeared, at best guess, to be a thick blanket of trees marching along in a never ending row. There was a heavy mist, and it was impossible to see more than twenty metres ahead. It seemed as though there was nothing between themselves and the dark outlines except flat ground wreathed in swirling mists and shifting shadows. Harriet shivered. She was freezing, but her involuntary shudder was not entirely from cold. She debated the wisdom of walking in the dark, drenched and frozen to the core. To add to the atmosphere, Harriet felt uneasy – as if she were being watched. A shiver went down her spine, and she shifted fractionally closer to Gideon. He was solid, comfortable and familiar, albeit sodden and frozen himself. They really had no choice but to keep moving, no matter how she felt – the trees had to be warmer than this open, frosty wasteland.

Their feet squelched in their shoes as they trudged across the empty land towards the tree line. The forest loomed nearer and eventually, through the cloying mist, they could see a faint glow. It was barely there, but they fixed on it and walked straight toward it by unspoken agreement. They were too cold and tired to do anything else. Both knew that spending more time exposed to the cold and fog could spell disaster.

As Harriet and Gideon neared the source of the light, the glow grew brighter. They moved forward together, clinging close to each other's side without consciously realising that they had shifted closer to one another. The light seemed to shift, drawing them towards it – towards whatever was waiting for them at the other end. As one, Harriet and Gideon traversed the last section of the moor and as they crossed into the trees, the clinging mist seemed to lift away from their shoulders. They were still freezing, but their hike across the barren landscape had warmed them enough to keep them moving forwards, no matter how slowly. Encouraged by the warmth of the forest, Harriet and Gideon wound their way through the trees that appeared to be ancient. Deeper and deeper into the forest they went, the impossibly tall trees surrounding them and reaching high into the sky. They went around ancient trunks so huge it would take more than just the two of them with their arms outstretched to reach around them. The ground was covered in green moss and thick leaves. It was like something out of a fairy tale, and it demanded enthrallment – or at least it would have, if they hadn't been facing imminent death or, at the very least, permanent injury from frostbite.

Without warning, Harriet and Gideon tumbled into a clearing that resembled an enchanting fairy garden. The grass was thick and green on the ground and there were picturesque logs dotted around the circular clearing. In the middle stood an enormous, imposing tree, even more grand than the ones they had already admired. And in front of it, standing tall against the beauty that was the wizened trunk of an impossibly old tree, was a sight that made them both stop in their tracks. Gideon's eyes widened. Harriet exclaimed in fear and took an involuntary step back as they took in the tableau before them.

Three women stood on the other side of a fire burning in the middle of the clearing, each one more beautiful than the last. They turned to look at Harriet and Gideon as they stood glued to the spot in the fringe of trees surrounding the clearing.

"Ah, our wait has ended," said the middle of the three, her pale beauty ethereal and stunning. Mesmerising. The fire that crackled, and the warmth of it, called to a thoroughly bedraggled and chilled Harriet, luring her towards its comfort. She desperately wanted to get closer to it, needing its warmth to heat her frozen flesh. But she didn't dare to move, either forwards or backwards.

"Come, be warm," the second woman said, her stunning beauty almost other worldly. She beckoned them towards the fire, and it seemed as though its warm embrace reached out its arms to caress and tempt them closer.

"You must be so cold," the third said, her voice light and tinkling. "Come now, be comfortable." She too was gorgeous, as unparalleled in beauty as her sisters. Each moved with a grace that made them appear as though they were walking on air, not quite touching the ground as mere mortals would.

Harriet could feel Gideon's reaction, and it matched her own. She was afraid, yet entranced and comforted at the same time. She sensed that these women were not a threat, but there was no logic as to how or why she knew that. Harriet moved first, unable to resist the lure of the fire that promised to warm her and save her from hypothermia. Gideon followed seconds later, as if they were parts of the same person connected by strings. They stuck closely together, finding safety and comfort in their proximity, despite not feeling any real danger from the three sisters.

"Ye clothes willnae do," the first sister remarked, studying the bedraggled pair standing before her. She turned around and stooped down. As she straightened, Harriet saw a bundle of dry clothes in her arms. She almost cried out with relief. There were blankets too.

The dazzlingly beautiful woman glided across the clearing, her arms outstretched. In a daze, Harriet and Gideon took the clothes they were offered.

"There now," the first sister murmured. "I can feel yer anticipation at bein warm again."

"She is the one who carries the book," the second sister said, as if in conversation with her kin.

"She is the one we have been waiting fer," the third sister chimed in.

"I'm the…what now?" Harriet said, ruthlessly quashing the stammer from her voice. These women clearly had some sort of power, and they wielded it as effortlessly as they moved.

She certainly wasn't in Tasmania anymore.

Gideon still looked stunned, and he was looking from the sisters to Harriet and back again.

Harriet racked her brains, trying to remember anything from a Shakespearean play she'd read recently that might help. God help her if this had nothing to do with Shakespeare – his life and the worlds he had created were all she had immersed herself in for months now. But there was so much to remember. Where to start?

"The spirits have foretold yer arrival," she chanted, floating around the fire in the centre of the clearing, moving closer to the trio.

"They have?" Harriet asked, her tone casual despite how madly her insides churned.

"Yes. We are in times of great turmoil. There are men – great men – who listen fer portents, rely on prophecies, but hear what they wish ter hear. We need yer ter stop the bloodshed."

Harriet glanced at Gideon uneasily. He still seemed entranced, as if he wasn't entirely listening to what was going on.

"What is it that I'm supposed to do?" Harriet asked with a sense of impending doom.

"We are sisters four. But oor last sister has chosen a dark and dangerous road. Even more dangerous for the one she controls," the second sister said.

"Ye must find her, and stop her," the third sister continued. "Despite oor power, we cannae. She is of oor blood."

"If she succeeds," the first sister warned, "she will wipe out the power behind the throne of Scotland. All who come after will suffer. At the end of the solstice, after time moves into a new rotation around the sun, t'will be too late. Find her, stop her, and when the stars align, ye will have yer reward."

The three sisters melted into the dark forest surrounding the clearing, leaving no trace that they had been there in the first place.

Gideon shook his dark head, confusion clear on his face. It was like Harriet was watching him wake from a daydream.

"What just happened?" Gideon asked, a frown on his face. "Did you see them too?"

"Yes," Harriet said, putting her bundle of clothes down on a nearby log. "Now you need to turn around while I get these clothes off."

Gideon looked at the pile in his own arms as if seeing them for the first time. "Where did these come from?" He murmured. Then he glanced up at Harriet, waiting for him to avert his eyes.

"Oh, sorry," he mumbled, rapidly turning his back. Harriet waited a moment before she unbuttoned her jacket pocket and took the book out. It was definitely dry. Harriet sighed with relief, then quickly stripped off her sodden clothes. She felt the heavy, cold, dragging sensation of her wet clothes leave her and her skin heat as she wrapped herself in a rough blanket. Harriet moved towards the fire, lured by the welcoming blaze. Folding her wet clothes, she looked around before stashing them inside the hollow of an imposing tree. Perfect. Scooping up the book, she sat down on a log beside the fire, tweaking the blanket to make sure that her skin was as covered as it could possibly be.

"I'm done," Harriet called out to Gideon, whose back was still turned. He swivelled around, then stopped dead when he saw Harriet wearing nothing but a blanket. A blush rose in his cheeks and he averted his eyes.

"I need to wait until I'm dry before I put the new clothes on," Harriet explained. "You will too." Gideon nodded, but Harriet could still see the little spark of panic in his eyes. She smirked a little.

Before long, Gideon was seated on the log to the left of Harriet's. He had been so quick she'd barely had time to think through what she knew, or at least suspected. Which admittedly, wasn't a great deal.

"Do you have any idea where we are? Or who those women were?" Gideon asked, his brow furrowed in concentration. "The more I try to remember, the harder it is to hold onto the details."

Harriet shrugged in response. That was interesting. She remembered everything that had happened with crystal clear clarity. Perhaps the three sisters had done something to Gideon's memory – perhaps it was the cold. Harriet poked at the pile of brown beside her: she saw what looked like soft leather shoes, and a dark, non-descript dress made of rough material. Peeking out from underneath the brown was a forest green cloak that looked warm and inviting. It would certainly be more comfortable than the coarse blanket she was wearing. And besides, Harriet was undoubtedly drier and warmer than she had been an hour ago. Getting dressed would also give her an excellent excuse to avoid Gideon's questions.

Gesturing for him to turn around again, which he did without complaint, Harriet took her time pulling the brown dress over her head and tying the laces up. She slipped the leather shoes onto her feet and draped the forest green cloak, which was actually very beautiful, over the top of her dress. Harriet was grateful for the hood that hid her hair, still drying from their dip in the river. Whichever one it had turned out to be in the end. And her mother had been wrong – a dip in the Derwent hadn't washed the rebellious red from her hair.

Trading places with Gideon, Harriet sat back down and stared broodingly into the fire. This had to have something to do with a time rift. There were no modern inventions in sight, and the clothes that she had been given were rougher and plainer than the ones she, or even Caterina, had worn in Verona. Her hypothesis was confirmed when Gideon came back into view, dressed in the clothes that had been left for him. Harriet couldn't help it – she burst out laughing.

"What am I wearing?" Gideon asked with a grin, spreading his arms wide and spinning around slowly like a male model. "Whatever it is, I'm rocking it."

Harriet shook with laughter, mirth wreathing her face. Her laughter was stopped abruptly by the sound of clinking metal, and she was stunned as an arrow flew uncomfortably close to her face before thudding into the ancient tree in the centre of the clearing. Gideon's eyes widened, and he instinctively moved closer to

Harriet, attempting to shield her from the threat that had materialised in the idyllic clearing.

"Explain yeselves," came a harsh voice. "Before I put the next arrow through yer heart."

Chapter Six

Harriet and Gideon watched in horror as a young man came into the clearing, followed by ten men armed to the teeth with swords, bows and arrows. They were all dressed in much the same way as Gideon, although on a grander scale. Each wore close fitting pants – leggings, even – with a longer tunic over the top. Belts were slung around their waists and holstered many of their weapons. The necks of their shirts were open, exposing their throats.

Except for the leader, the man who had let the arrow fly. He wore a leather vest over the top of his tunic, designed to protect him and show his status as the man in charge.

"I'm waitin," the leader growled, notching another arrow into his bow.

"Wait, wait," Gideon said, holding out his hand. The leader arched an eyebrow at him and drew the bow string taut.

"We're runaways," Harriet blurted out, moving from behind Gideon. Thinking quickly, she seized Gideon's hand and held it. Ignoring the sparks she felt at the contact, Harriet ploughed on.

"We've run away from our families…they don't want us to be together." Harriet sighed, clutching Gideon's hand both for support and to stop him from contradicting her tale. "We wish to marry, and so we've left our home in search of another who will accept us." Harriet wasn't exactly improvising – she was stealing Juliet's story verbatim.

"A pretty tale," the leader said, dropping his arrow fractionally. "Where is ye home?"

"Near England," Harriet improvised, trying to think of somewhere that would explain their accents. The arrow rose immediately and was trained on Harriet's heart. She held her breath.

"The English are no friends of oors," the leader growled, his voice sounding menacing despite his age. "Give me one good reason why I shouldna put this arrow through ye right now."

"My Lord," said one of the leader's men. He put his head close to his master, and whispered something in his ear.

"Och yes!" The leader grunted. He turned his gaze back to Harriet and Gideon. "That will work better. You two! Yer coming with us."

Harriet looked at Gideon, bewildered. He stared back, unsure of what to do.

The man in charge narrowed his eyes, his wild beard and hair adding to his menacing presence. "Yer my prisoners now. Ye will fetch a pretty ransom when yer families petition the King o' England ter get yer back. Get up. Ye've got a ways ter walk."

***

"He wasn't kidding," Harriet mumbled to Gideon as they trudged through the dark. Their hands were tied in front of their bodies, and they had been lashed together and attached to a long rope that extended up to the saddle of the young man's horse. "How long have we been walking for now? It must be hours."

Gideon didn't reply, he just kept up the steady pace they'd followed for what felt like an age. Harriet was grateful for the boots the sisters had given her, and for the cloak that swirled around her ankles as she walked. The hood kept the frost off her head and cast her face in shadows. When she had first travelled back in time, she had been riding the horse instead of being tied to it. She still wasn't overly comfortable around the animals, and these ones looked wilder, more primitive, than Juliet and Caterina's horses had been in Verona. She suppressed a shudder. Despite the hard walk, she was glad she was on her feet instead of up behind the huge, hulking animal. Though that could change the longer they traipsed through the dead of the night.

"Look at that star cluster," Gideon murmured, nodding his head up and to the right. Harriet stared in disbelief. The man was looking at stars at a time like this? But she followed his motions and gazed up at the sky, which provided an inky black, velvety background for the millions of brilliant balls that burned brightly. As she saw what he meant, she frowned. Gideon was right. It didn't take a stargazer to see that there was a pattern glowing in the sky that wasn't usually there, and it was in the same three stars they had seen on the banks of the Derwent.

"What do you think they are?" Harriet whispered.

'I've never seen that before," Gideon replied. "And I like stars, so I've studied them a fair bit. That's not a constellation I know about."

The stars in question were in a circular pattern, an intricate radiation of light that created a stunning effect on the watcher. In the centre of the pattern was the most unusual part of the constellation. One star, brilliant in its depth, burned a bright blue colour. Light and dark blue seemed to pulse through it, producing the effect of a living organism. It was as though blood pulsed through the star, giving it life. It flickered between light and dark – between brilliant illumination and shadowy beauty. Beneath it sat the two fainter blue stars, just as they had in Tasmania. Except, if you looked closely, they were slightly off centre. The bright star looked as though it had flowered, its brilliance extending out beyond its radiant centre.

"I've never seen it either," Harriet whispered. "It's beautiful." Looking up as she was, Harriet didn't see the uneven ground before her until she stumbled and almost fell. Gideon caught her with his forearms, standing her upright and dragging her along simultaneously so they didn't attract the attention of their captors. Harriet resumed her trudging pace, a little breathless from the contact with Gideon. She was glad he wasn't a big talker. Or didn't seem to be, anyway. Harriet wasn't sure how long she could have pretended to have absolutely no idea what was happening to them before she cracked. True, she did have relatively little idea what was going on, but she would wager that she knew more than Gideon did. They definitely hadn't travelled to Verona again…the air felt different here. The sky seemed closer and a little more confining. They certainly weren't looking at the soaring and boundless skies of Australia. And it was far too brisk and foggy to be their homeland. Their clothes, and those of the men who had captured them, pointed to a time earlier than Juliet and Caterina's. That had been the 14th century. As they walked, Harriet racked her mind for anything she knew about history prior to the 14th century. Had she read any plays, books – even textbooks – that might help them discover where they were. She'd been focussing heavily on Shakespeare, trying to decipher the connection between herself and the old playwright. Harriet supposed that there was some way they were linked, and that hypothesis would only be further proven if they had indeed gone back into another of his plays.

The drawing mustn't be the portal, Harriet thought ruefully. She didn't have it with her. It was still tucked into her suitcase back in the rented cabin. So if that wasn't it – what was? The book? Impossible. She didn't know the book had existed until the trip to Richmond.

Harriet was pulled from her fractured thoughts as the men seated on their horses in front of them stopped abruptly. They could hear murmuring amongst the men, but not what they were saying. Their accents were strong and Harriet had been trying to place them as they walked. Scottish, perhaps? That was another clue that might help. They had mentioned the English King, and wanting to ransom them back to him. Did that mean they were dealing with an enemy of the English monarchy? Were they in England, or somewhere else? It seemed reasonable that they were close enough for England to be a major player in whatever was happening here, and the climate supported that. Something elusive – some memory or fragment of imagining – was skating around the edges of Harriet's mind. She couldn't quite grasp it, and so couldn't do anything with it. Harriet knew it was essential to understand whatever it was, but just couldn't focus her concentration enough to achieve it.

An unearthly scream rent the air, and both Harriet and Gideon exclaimed in surprise as the young leader's horse suddenly reared high up into the air, trying to throw its rider and snorting in fear. The leader's mount wheeled to face them and they could see the whites of its eyes, wide and staring in the dark of the night. Standing as they were on the moors,

Harriet and Gideon were hideously exposed. They had not long quit the forest and the encompassing trees that seemed to stretch forever. And they were tied up…if the beast decided to bolt, it wouldn't end well for them. Harriet could see the horse's distress from where she stood, frozen to the spot. She didn't know what had caused it, but could see the leader trying to calm his mount, stroking her neck and speaking soothingly to her in a language they couldn't understand.

"I told you 'tis bad luck to shoot at the Birnam Oak," one of the men exclaimed irritably, fear and superstition written over his face. "You hit it dead on."

"Tis not the work of magic," the leader growled, sweat beading on his face from his attempts to keep his horse controlled. "She simply spooked, tis all." The horse was finally starting to calm. Luckily, none of the other horses had taken fright and were standing steadily, waiting for their fellow animal to stop panicking. The apprehension on the leader's face showed that despite his words, there might be enough truth in the superstition of divine retribution to make him uneasy. He looked contemplatively at his two captives.

"You," he lifted his chin to indicate Harriet. "Ye will go up behind Aiden." The chosen man nodded, then jumped down from his horse to stride over to where Harriet and Gideon stood.

"The man will ride with me," the leader declared. Gideon looked a little pale in the moonlight – Harriet supposed she would as well if she has been ordered to get onto the creature that had so recently tried to rid herself of her master. On the upside, they wouldn't be walking for a while now.

Aiden made short work of their bonds, keeping Harriet and Gideon's hands tied but removing the ropes that bound them together. When they were no longer tethered to the leader's saddle, Gideon made his way to the side of the spooked horse. Harriet was led back to the dappled white stallion Aiden called his own. She could see Gideon glancing over at her uneasily – it seemed as though he didn't want to be separated from her. She felt much the same way.

Harriet didn't have long to think about how she was going to clamber atop the horse, as Aiden grabbed her around the waist and simply threw her up onto his saddle. Harriet scrambled frantically, trying to gain purchase on the slippery leather. The stirrups swung wildly as she wriggled her way up onto the horse's back in her dress and cloak. She could sense the amusement of the men watching on, and it infuriated her. Righting herself, she put her chin in the air and looked down on them with an air of haughtiness. Aiden grinned and vaulted into the saddle in front of her.

As much as Harriet wanted to maintain her air of detached calm, she squeaked as the horse started to move and grabbed at Aiden to remain seated. He shook with laughter, but was wise enough to remain silent.

"We will move faster," the leader declared, glancing around at the fog wreathing the moors. "Be cautious with yer horses in the dark."

Emboldened by her position up behind Aiden, Harriet turned her attention to the man in charge of their capture and imprisonment. She didn't feel as vulnerable, now that she wasn't physically tethered to him.

"I demand to know the name of our captor," Harriet declared, trying to inject authority into her voice. The leader regarded her steadily, and Harriet could sense Gideon watching her quietly from the back of his saddle.

"Tis Lachlan," he replied quietly, before spurring his horse into motion and leading his men into the night.

Harriet's world spun on its axis once more. Lachlan. The scrawled writing in the book blazed across her memory, like a sparkler making its mark on a dark night. It couldn't be a coincidence...could it?

Chapter Seven

The sun had snuck up over the horizon before Harriet, lulled to sleep by the rhythmic rocking of the horse, awoke with a start. She rubbed her eyes, then looked again at her surroundings.

Gone were the mists and fogs of the night before. In the dark, the landscape had appeared foreboding and sparse. In the brilliant sunshine, it was vastly different. The landscape ahead of them was gorgeously green. Everything was fresh and smelled wonderfully of clean air and earth. There were miles and miles of purple waves, swaying slightly in thc breeze as the flowers on the heather opened up to the sun. The landscape was rugged – hills and outcrops barred them from making their way directly from one point to another. Harriet wasn't fond of the way the horse pitched forward as he made his way down an embankment, or tipped Harriet so far backwards that it felt as though she would drop off his hindquarters.

As they rounded the bend of a rocky outcrop, Harriet saw the sweep of the terrain in front of them, and despite their danger, it caught at her heart. There was flat land for acres, and in the middle of all that space stood a hill with gradually sloping sides and a castle perched atop it. The castle was imposing – grand even, yet Harriet instinctively knew that she wasn't looking at the most splendid abode this land had to offer.

"Dunsinane," Aiden murmured, gesturing to the castle with his chin. It was the first time Harriet had heard him speak since she had gone up behind him on his horse the night before.

Although the sunlight was currently showering down upon them, it wasn't the only thing that would be raining down before this trip was over. Harriet could see the clouds gathering on the horizon, and so could Lachlan.

"Yer to travel faster," he growled, flicking his hand toward the open space that stretched endlessly between where they stood and the slopes of the castle hill. Kicking his horse, Lachlan took off at a gallop, Gideon clinging to his saddle.

Aiden followed suit, and Harriet seized the back of his tunic in a death grip. She was bounced around unceremoniously, constricted by the skirts of her dress and the length of her cloak. It was a rough and bumpy ride – not something that Harriet looked forward to repeating any time soon. She hung on grimly, constantly checking and calculating the distance they had left to travel before they reached the castle. It couldn't come soon enough. Harriet was beginning to feel distinctly green.

They began to climb steadily as the terrain became steeper, hillier, rockier. They wound their way towards the entrance to the castle on the hill, the beaten earth tracks muddy with footprints and churned up by the passage of many horses.

As the sun soared high in the sky and the thunderclouds raced across to block its rays, they reached the front gates of Dunsinane Castle. Lachlan turned his horse to observe his men, and his prisoners. Harriet glared back at him defiantly. She glanced at Gideon's face – he was looking a little sick after their race across the purple fields, too. Lachlan grunted and turned back to the walls of the castle.

The huge wooden gates were closed firmly against the outside world, cutting Dunsinane off from the surrounding land and villages. Lachlan reached out and tugged on the long rope beside the gates, and a clanging began somewhere behind the fortified walls. He silently eyed Harriet as he waited for a response. She fought to keep her face impassive.

A man had come running from inside the keep of the castle, and a window was thrown open beside the gate.

"Master Lachlan!" he declared, affection clear in his tone. Harriet stared. How could anyone possibly like the man who held them captive.

"Alasdair," Lachlan nodded his head. "Found these two here near the Birnam Oak. English, or so they say. We'll hold them as prisoners fer ransom." Alasdair looked up at Gideon, perched on the back of Lachlan's horse. Then his gaze switched to Harriet, and he looked a little troubled.

"Is my Father here yet?" Lachlan asked.

"Ach Master Lachlan," the man exclaimed. "Ye Father is here, and he'll be right chuffed to see ye, wee barra!"

"Belter!" Lachlan cried. "Yer must fetch my Father. He will know how ter handle this pair."

"Of course. Bide ye time, I will summon him now," the man exclaimed. "Just give me a moment."

Lachlan shifted impatiently on his horse as the wooden window was slammed shut and the man's footsteps echoed into the heart of the keep, and presumably the castle. But they had hardly faded into the still, pre-storm air before a flurry of boots rang on the stones within the walls of the castle. The window was flung open again. A middle aged man with dark hair, a salt and pepper beard and wise, kind eyes peered out through the portal.

"Speak o' the Devil!" the voice that went with the face thundered out from behind the fortified walls. "It's about time ye showed yer face, Lachlan." The wise eyes swept over Harriet and Gideon, noting the ropes that restrained them.

"Ye look like yer in a right situation," Lachlan's father said. "Explain yeself, before it turns as black as the Earl of Hell's waistcoat out there."

Large parts of the strongly Scottish language went straight over Harriet's head, and she didn't think Gideon was doing any better at following the conversation. They had no idea what was happening.

Before long, Lachlan and his father appeared to reach an agreement. Harriet and Gideon were escorted into the keep of the castle, which stood as an imposing grey stone monolith rising out of the hillside before them. Although it had seemed quiet from the outside, the area in front and around the castle was a hive of activity. And it was bigger than it looked from the exterior. As the horses were led to the stables, Harriet watched the women scurrying back and forth among the various outbuildings in the keep. It was like a shanty town of sorts.

The inhabitants of the castle stared furtively at the newcomers, peering curiously at the ropes that held their wrists tight. When Harriet looked down, she could see that the ropes had burned her wrists, leaving red welts where they had rubbed her skin raw.

Although their captor was relatively gentle in hauling them along, they could hear from the discussion between father and son that their immediate fate wouldn't be all that pleasant.

"The dungeons are out, I'm afraid," Lachlan's father said, his black eyebrow raised as he watched his son's face. He glanced back briefly at Harriet and Gideon, then looked forward again. Lachlan's father clearly wasn't disposed to helping them out of their imprisonment.

Father and son exchanged comments and suggestions, their accents firing their words back and forth, before they finally settled on an airless room with no windows. It appeared to be a secondary chamber off what must be the cellars for the castle.

Harriet and Gideon were thrust unceremoniously into the small chamber.

"Yer to stay here until we decide what ter do with ye," Lachlan growled, his face contrasting with his manner. His features were smooth and unlined – clearly the face of a youth just a little older than they were. But his voice and actions belied those of a much older man – one who had been groomed to lead. They watched helplessly as Lachlan kicked the door closed, and listened as the bolt scraped across the door, ending with a loud clunk. The sound of rattling keys taunted them as Lachlan's footsteps stalked back up the winding stone stairs they had been hauled down.

Harriet sat down gingerly on a rough wooden pallet that looked like it was used to hold crates of something. It didn't collapse under her weight, and for that she was grateful. Gideon crossed to the door, pushing and pulling against the solid timber. He twisted and turned the metal ring pull, but the door didn't move an inch. Resigned, he sighed and turned to face Harriet.

"It was worth a try, at least," he said, sitting heavily on a squat, round barrel. They'd barely had time to exchange two words since their ordeal had begun, and Harriet was acutely aware that it would be hard to avoid Gideon's questions in their makeshift prison. From sodden and freezing, to warm and enchanted and finally, to captives, the last 24 hours had been a whirlwind for them both. On their forced trek, Harriet had plenty of time to think about what was happening now, and the parallels to what she had experienced a bare six months before. Frowning, Harriet calculated. Actually, it had been exactly six months before that she had found herself in sunny Verona – about as far away from this cold, beautiful land as one could get.

"Where are we?" Gideon grated out, raking his hands through his dark hair. He gripped his head before pulling his fingers free of the shiny locks.

"I don't know," Harriet responded, rather lamely. She had several ideas, but each of them would seem insane to the young man trapped down in the cellars with her.

"It's like we went through some sort of…I don't know…portal?" Gideon said, scrunching up his face in concentration. "The last thing I remember seeing before we went under the water were the stars hovering on the horizon. I was looking for you, and I ducked my head under to see better." Gideon trailed off.

"When we came back up, we were clearly somewhere else," Harriet continued.

"But...how?" Gideon asked, perplexed. "How can we possibly be somewhere completely different? It makes no sense. We're obviously not even in the same time period. Look at me! These are the clothes the women in the forest gave me." Gideon stood and held out his arms. Despite their predicament, Harriet felt a bubble of laughter rising up in her throat again. She ruthlessly quashed it.

"At least you're good at thinking on your feet," Gideon said, kicking his toe against the barrel in disgust.

"What do you mean?" Harriet asked, her head tilted to the side. She tended to get distracted in Gideon's presence, and that would only get harder now that they were locked together in a room no bigger than her bathroom at home.

"When the arrow hit the tree, I couldn't think straight. But you...that story about us running away from our families – that was something else. And it worked. How did you think of that on the spot?" Gideon sat back down on his barrel seat, propping his head up on his hand.

"Ah...it was nothing," Harriet said weakly.

How could she tell Gideon that she'd stolen the plotline straight from the last story she'd popped into? Because it was seeming exceedingly likely that she'd burst into another one, this time with an unexpected, and not entirely unwelcome, companion.

"Lachlan said he's going to ransom us back to the English King when our families petition to get us back," Gideon said, frowning. "So…what happens when our families don't do that?"

Yes…that was a problem. And Harriet had no answer.

She was longing to tell Gideon about her trip to Verona. Who knew, maybe he would spot something that might help. But he'd also think she was a freak. He might not even believe her. Harriet tried to think about how she would react if their positions were reversed. She would struggle to believe it at first…but then, so had Juliet and Caterina. And they'd come around quite quickly. In addition, Gideon was in a world that he knew nothing about, wearing clothes that made him look like Robin Hood hundreds of years before his time. Neither of them understood where they were or why, and it would be much less lonely to share her suspicions and thoughts with Gideon than it would be to keep him in the dark. He might think she was crazy, but she'd have to deal with that when they got home. If they did.

"Our families clearly won't ransom us…I doubt they know where we are. I got the idea to tell Lachlan that we'd run away from another story. It was about two teenagers who were in love, but couldn't be together because they were from enemy houses. I'd…heard about it." Innate caution made her hesitate at the last minute. She shook her head, exasperated with our own cowardice. She opened her mouth, preparing herself for the worst.

"Oh yeah!" Gideon frowned in concentration. "Now that you mention it, that's Romeo and Juliet! We did that last year at school. No wonder it seemed familiar."

Well. That had been easier than expected. Harriet and Gideon lapsed into awkward silence.

Harriet fished in her cloak for the book that had travelled alongside them. Gideon had seen it when they'd come out of the river, but he hadn't paid it much mind since. He had been sufficiently distracted by the appearance of the three sisters, then the drama of their forced march through the countryside.

Harriet thumbed through the pages as Gideon got up to inspect their makeshift prison, poking at crates and sniffing barrels as he went. Harriet gingerly moved through the book until she got to the section where she had seen Lachlan's name scrawled onto the parchment. It was on the page that had Macbeth scribbled in what had once been bold, black ink at the top. Beneath were faded words, some illegible other than a few scratchings here and there. Harriet could pick out a few letters on some, and whole names or descriptions on others.

Lachlan, Macbeth, Scottish battle, King, crown, English, Dunca, witc were the words, or mostly words, that Harriet could decipher. She recognised Macbeth as another of Shakespeare's works, but she realised with a sinking feeling of despair that this was one of his tales she knew little about. In fact, she knew next to nothing.

Sighing with frustration, Harriet slammed the book closed.

"What's that?" Gideon asked curiously as he rounded the corner of the small space he had squeezed in to investigate.

"It's a book I found, back in the town we were staying in," Harriet answered. She saw no reason to hide its existence – even she couldn't see a clear connection to her own predicament – ability – whatever it was that kept sending her through time rifts.

"May I see?" Gideon asked, his interest piqued. Harriet handed over the book, and Gideon took it with a low whistle. "It's certainly old," he said, turning it over in his hands. "I'd say perhaps from around the late 16th century or so. Maybe even the 17th century."

"How do you know that?" Harriet asked, tilting her head curiously.

"I like old things," Gideon replied with a shrug. He opened the book and looked inside, thumbing through the pages carefully. His face became more animated, more excited, as Harriet watched him absorb the contents of the pages.

"This looks like a list – a sketch of sorts – of Shakespeare's works. Look! There's Romeo and Juliet, including the characters and the location of the book. Here's Othello…that was a good read. Ah Macbeth. I love that story." Then Gideon frowned. He turned the book around so that Harriet could see it.

"See here, it says Lachlan," Gideon said, excitement in his voice. "There is no Lachlan in the original story of Macbeth. I wonder how that got in there? Maybe he was written out of the original text?"

Harriet leaned forward, her arms on her thighs. "So…you're telling me that you know something about Shakespeare?"

Gideon frowned. "Just because I play sport doesn't mean I'm a dumb jock," he replied, some of the excitement leaching from his voice.

Harriet paled. "Oh, I didn't mean it that way," she said quickly. But the damage had been done.

"Everyone sees me that way," Gideon said bitterly. "I'm just the fullback of the football team, the captain of the soccer team. No one thinks I could possibly have a brain – not even my own parents. My father has forced me into sport for as long as I can remember. Don't get me wrong, I love to play. But there's more to me than just being a footy player."

Harriet looked at Gideon through distressed eyes. She'd tapped into a deep well of feeling that lurked close to the surface, and the poison from that hurt had spilled out into the space they were both trapped in. Gideon had turned his body away fractionally, just enough for Harriet to notice the change. He was closing off from her – she had seen her brothers do it when she'd hurt their feelings in the past.

Harriet had made a serious misstep, although she hadn't intended to. The only thing that worked with her brothers in these situations was to show them how much she cared for them, and that she trusted and respected them. Harriet definitely wasn't prepared to show Gideon just how much she cared about him…even she didn't really know that. But she could show him that she trusted him. It could cost her everything, but so could being locked in a cellar until Lord Whatshisface decided to release them. Or didn't. She could always petition her parents to move States if this went south, and they managed to find their way back home.

Harriet took a deep breath, and she grimaced. "Gideon, I know you're more than just a footy player. I'm glad that you're here with me, going through this with me, because of that. You see…I haven't been completely honest with you."

Gideon was completely absorbed, his jaw hanging open slackly, as Harriet told him about her trip back to Verona, into Romeo and Juliet, six months before. She told him everything – it all came flooding out in a rush of pent up emotion and feeling. It was what she had wanted to talk to someone – anyone – about since she had returned, but she hadn't had anyone to share it with. Thankfully she hadn't told Tessa, given all that had transpired since. The thought of Gracie and what she had done to her life left Harriet with a bad taste in the mouth, and she forced her attention back to Gideon.

Whose face registered stunned amazement.

"I guess it's pretty unbelievable," Harriet finished lamely, turning the book she had retrieved from Gideon over in her hands.

"Well…ordinarily it would be hard to swallow," Gideon said slowly. "But given where we are…it's a little easier to believe than you would think. If you say that's what happened, I believe you."

Harriet brightened, buoyed by Gideon's trust. They discussed her time in Verona in more depth. Gideon was fascinated, hanging on Harriet's every word. Both were looking for a clue to explain how they came to be in this strange land and time – even something that might confirm where they actually were now.

"So…you just woke up in Juliet's bedroom?" Gideon asked.

"Yes," Harriet confirmed. "And I woke up in my own when I came back. I wasn't asleep when I left Verona though." She frowned. "It's sort of like I woke up back where I would have been had I not travelled at all."

"That makes sense," Gideon agreed. He looked like he was about to say something else, when they both heard the fall of heavy footsteps on the circular staircase down to their prison. Both stopped talking and stared at each other, before shifting slightly closer together and staring at the door.

The heavy steps stopped just outside the door, and it swung open without ceremony. Lachlan's scowling face came into view.

"Yer to dine with us this evening in the hall. At the servant's table, mind. And yer'll be back down here in a jiffy if yer so much as think about escapin'. Come with me." Lachlan's voice rang with command. Harriet and Gideon both stood, and Harriet slipped the book unobtrusively into her cloak as she moved behind Gideon to the doorway.

"Just one wrong move," Lachlan said, his voice cold. "And yer'll spend the rest o' yer lives down here."

They believed him.

Chapter Eight

The rowdy laughter of a hundred people filled the cavernous hall of Dunsinane Castle. The lords, including the man they knew to be Lachlan's father, had been served their meals at what was obviously the head table. Instead of the individually plated dinner Harriet was used to receiving at home, the trestle tables set up around the hall were laden with dishes of different meals. Those seated around the tables were chatting animatedly as they took what they wanted from each platter. There was an empty place to the left of Lachlan's father, and they watched Lachlan stalk up to claim it from the seats he had thrust them into at the end of a long table. Harriet watched the exchange between father and son keenly. It seemed from their gestures that Lachlan's father might be responsible for Harriet and Gideon's meal tonight.

If how the meals were served in this time seemed different to them, the food on the servers along the table was even more foreign to anything either of them had eaten before. Perched on a hard bench with what appeared to be household servants, Harriet and Gideon seemed to be choosing from the discarded dishes of the main table. Gideon had already started eating – tearing into the food, really – and Harriet could feel her stomach roiling with hunger. She took a piece of meat and examined it, before falling back on the old belief that if you didn't dwell on it long enough, everything tasted like chicken.

The hall was lit by the flames of hundreds of candles. Torches blazed in the brackets on the walls and there were huge iron chandeliers above their heads. The kitchen servants and maids who weren't eating darted back and forth from the scullery, serving the increasingly drunken lords and their men occupying the castle dining tables.

There was a lady beside Lachlan's father, and Harriet's eyes were inexorably drawn to her. It seemed that she couldn't look away. The lady was haughtily beautiful. Her raven black hair was pinned back so that her alabaster skin, not at all ravaged by age, was the centrepiece of her lovely face. Her big, dark eyes took in her surroundings shrewdly, even if the men surrounding her didn't notice it.

Harriet watched under her eyelashes as the lady leaned her dark head towards Lachlan's father, and he listened attentively to her words. He glanced over at Harriet and Gideon, then back down at the table. He nodded his dark head.

Harriet glanced further along the table and saw that Lachlan and his family weren't seated in pride of place. That position was occupied by an older man, dressed in splendour that could only belie someone of great importance. His shoulders were draped in fur, and his tunic seemed of a finer quality than the many other men dotted around the hall. It was even more remarkable than those of the men who sat with him at the head table. As Harriet watched, she saw the man turn his greying head to reveal a glint of gold. Above his lined face was the mark of monarchy – the crown of what must be the Kings of the country they were in.

Around them, the sound of people conversing ebbed and flowed. Many of the discussions they could hear were difficult to follow – the participants seemed to speak with a strong accent that was difficult to decipher at times. Although Lachlan didn't talk often, they had heard the same accent in his voice, albeit not as strong. Harriet hadn't been able to place it

– she had never heard a similar way of speaking before.

"That was delicious," Gideon said, sitting back a little from the long table. "Although, I was starving." They had both been remarkably hungry after their forced march through the unfamiliar countryside. When Harriet thought about it, neither had eaten since the evening before. Harriet was uncomfortably full now. She had the sick feeling in her stomach of eating too much too quickly. It made her sluggish, and she forced her mind to focus on any clues they could pick up from this outing. Who knew how long it would be before they were forced back downstairs to their airless prison.

"Don't look now," Gideon murmured in Harriet's ear. A shiver went down her spine at his unexpected proximity. "But Lachlan is making his way over here." Harriet suppressed the urge to look, and instead glanced up at the head table. Lachlan's father and the lady beside him were speaking with crowned man in the centre of the table.

Lachlan loomed beside them.

"My mother requests an audience with ye," he said stiffly, holding out his hand imperiously for Harriet's. Hesitating, Harriet glanced at Gideon. He grimaced and nodded slightly.

Harriet placed her hand in Lachlan's and allowed him to help her to her feet. It was harder than usual given the long skirts that swirled around her feet, restricting her ability to clamber over the bench. Gideon stood behind her and followed them closely.

"My mother says ter take yer to her sitting room," Lachlan said tersely. "Lord knows why," he muttered under his breath. As she was steered in that direction, with Gideon prowling in her wake, Harriet hoped that this was a positive intervention. Their situation could definitely be improved. It could also get worse.

Lachlan pushed open a door to his right. It swung back to reveal a comfortably appointed sitting room with a roaring fire in the corner. It was nowhere near as opulent as Juliet's castle in Verona, or as cozy as the cottage in Richmond, but it was warm and inviting despite the cold that had descended with the afternoon thunderstorm and the setting of the sun. They didn't have long to wait before Lachlan's mother joined them.

The lady's glittering midnight eyes were strangely mesmerising as they swept over Harriet and Gideon. Harriet watched as the lady swung the door shut and walked towards the fireplace.

"Sit, sit. Make yeselves comfortable," she invited. Harriet hesitated, as did Gideon. This was the exact opposite of the treatment they had come to expect in this time so far. Lachlan scowled in the corner, and Harriet wasn't sure what to make of his mother yet. Something in the pit of her stomach told her to tread carefully. That little voice of caution was usually accurate, so she listened to it. She caught Gideon's eye as they moved to sit, and mouthed the words, "Be careful." He nodded slightly to show he understood.

"My name is Gruoch," the lady continued as Harriet and Gideon seated themselves opposite to her. "Or Lady Macbeth, in a formal sense."

Harriet's world tilted as the familiar name dropped into the void between them. She could feel Gideon tense beside her – he had made the same connection.

"I am Harriet…Lady Hunter," Harriet replied in a measured, cautious tone. "And this is my…intended, Gideon…Lord White." Harriet could feel Gideon's surprise as she made up their titles, but he remained silent.

Lady Macbeth took some time to absorb that, clearly considering Harriet's accent and how it differed from her own. "Aye. Lachlan tells me that ye are run away from yer home," Lady

Macbeth replied, still taking the measure of each. Harriet stayed silent, merely inclining her head in agreement to Lady Macbeth's words.

"How did ye come to be in Scotland? In Birnam Wood? Lachlan says yer from England." Lady Macbeth's eyes glinted like obsidian gemstones in the flickering firelight. They glittered, bold and beautiful, and Harriet couldn't wrench her gaze away from them. It was unnerving, the way that she looked at them both. It was as if she could see through their evasiveness, through their cover story, all the way to their very souls. Harriet shivered.

"We are from a small town near England," Harriet improvised, trying her best to stick with what she had originally said. "We have left our homes to be married, as our families do not agree with our union. We had heard of…Scotland, and thought we might find help to be married here." Lady Macbeth laughed shortly. The sound was brusque and unnerving.

"Scotland is no place fer travellers just now," Lady Macbeth said, her eyes strangely cold and inviting at the same time. "Tis a wild place of conflict and unrest."

Excellent, Harriet thought. Just their luck that they had managed to fall right into the middle of a warring country. Last time it was families, this time it seemed it might be actual armies.

"And ye are all alone? A young pair in a strange land?" Lady Macbeth raised one eyebrow gracefully.

"We were, until we met Lachlan here," Harriet said, shifting Lady Macbeth's focus to her son. He grimaced in response.

"Aye, I have spoken with Lachlan about his manner," Lady Macbeth sighed. "Tis not what we usually do, taking prisoners. He was a little hasty, but with our kingdom the way it is just now…" Lady Macbeth spread her arms wide. A rueful look crossed her face.

"I suppose that's understandable," Harriet replied. "Are we to be kept as prisoners?"

"Nay," Lady Macbeth replied. "At least, not in the way that my son has said. But we cannae let ye go just now. The lands around Dunsinane, and our own home, is too dangerous ter travel just now."

"Is this not where you normally live?" Harriet asked, looking around the sitting room with its rich décor.

"Nay. We live at Inverness Castle," Lady Macbeth replied, settling back a fraction in her seat. "We have travelled from our lands ter see King Duncan, ter try and stop the unrest. Lachlan, of course, lives here, under the guidance of King Duncan. Tis tradition for firstborn sons to be trained by the reigning King," she continued. "My husband is King Duncan's cousin."

Interesting, Harriet mused.

"But ye will be tired from yer travels," Lady Macbeth said, rising fluidly from her seat. She moved with an elegant grace that seemed to be unconscious and innate. "Ye must rest. We'll speak again in the morning," Lady Macbeth said, leading them to the door of the sitting room. They moved with her, slightly dazed.

Lady Macbeth open the door onto the darkened hallway, leaned out slightly and retrieved one of the flaming torches from a wall sconce. She handed the light to Gideon.

"Ye room is up the stairs, at the start of the corridor and to the left. Tis not much, but tis better than the cellar." She smiled lightly before gliding back into the room, closing the door silently behind her.

Harriet and Gideon stood and stared at each other. What had just happened? Both felt dazed, as though a veil had just been lifted from their eyes. As with the sisters in the forest, Gideon seemed to be more affected.

"I can't remember a thing," he said irritably.

"I think she meant those stairs," Harriet whispered, pointing to a set of stone stairs at one end of the hallway, behind Gideon. They headed up the stone spiral staircase, the walls cold and hard to the touch. At the top they could see the door to the room they had been given, just as Lady Macbeth had described.

Gideon pulled on the door ring and it creaked open to reveal a room with one bed and little else. There was a fireplace, and beside it a single chair. Taking in the room, Harriet's face flamed red. There were two of them and only one bed. Could she really sleep beside Gideon White? Regardless of her trepidation and nerves she stepped inside, glad to be released from their cellar prison. In the end, Gideon solved her dilemma.

"I'll take the chair," he said, pointing to the corner near the fireplace. "You take the bed."

That didn't seem fair to Harriet, and she frowned. Sure, sleeping beside someone you have a massive crush on wouldn't be pleasant, but the chair did not look at all comfortable.

"Perhaps I should sleep in the chair, I'm lighter," Harriet said, though she wasn't very enthused by the idea. Gideon waved away her protest and went to inspect the furniture. Harriet closed the door softly behind them. It didn't take Gideon long to find a small stock of firewood, and he began to stack the logs in the grate to start a warming fire. The wind was howling through the long slits in the walls, and the temperature had plummeted significantly away from Lady Macbeth's sitting room. Harriet would be grateful for the warmth once the fire got going.

Before long it was crackling merrily in the hearth, and Gideon sat back on his heels to survey his handiwork. He pushed up to stand, and turned to face Harriet.

"I think we should go back over everything we know so far," he said, taking a seat on the edge of the bed. The chair was rock solid, and neither of them fancied sitting in it, let alone sleeping in it. Harriet knew that Gideon was likely to insist on it though.

"Okay," Harriet said, sitting cross-legged on the other side of the lumpy mattress. "We now know we're in Scotland."

"Yes," said Gideon, frowning. "If we follow the same logic as your last trip, no matter how we travelled, we're in another of Shakespeare's tales. Specifically, Macbeth. Lady Macbeth was a pretty strong clue, and alongside Lachlan's name being written in the book, I think it's pretty clear cut."

"But I don't know anything about Macbeth," Harriet wailed plaintively. "I read Henry VIII, and A Midsummer Night's Dream, but not Macbeth. I've been researching Shakespeare, looking for some clue as to how it is I travelled…," Harriet trailed off, frustrated that she hadn't been looking in the right direction.

"Ah," said Gideon, his eyes alight. "You might not have read Macbeth, but I have. And recently, too."

"That's fantastic!" Harriet said, her face lighting up. She faced Gideon eagerly. "What do you remember of the story?"

"Well," said Gideon, his eyes looking distant and focussed on his thoughts. "It's one of Shakespeare's tragedies. It's about greed, and lust for power. Duncan is the King of Scotland, and Macbeth one of his leaders. I'm not sure exactly what they're called here. Sort of like a Duke in the English monarchy, I suppose. Anyway, according to Shakespeare's version, Macbeth kills Duncan and takes the crown from him. Duncan's sons are disinherited: I think because they've fled the country. There's also a prophecy, delivered by witches in the woods. They say that Macbeth will become King, and that he will remain King until Birnham Wood comes to Dunsinane. Macbeth thinks that he is safe, because clearly that can't happen. A second prophecy also says that Macbeth can be killed by no man born of a woman. And again, as all men must be born of a woman, Macbeth thinks he can't be killed."

"It's a tragedy though," Harriet interjected. "So clearly there's a flaw somewhere here. Where's the 'but'?"

"That's just it," Gideon all but bounced in his eagerness to tell the tale. "MacDuff, a supporter of Duncan's son, Malcolm, restores his lord to the throne. As it turns out, MacDuff is ripped from his mother's stomach, so he is not technically born of a woman."

"Rubbish," Harriet snorted.

"Well yes, we know that," Gideon said. "But in this time, I suppose a caesarean birth would be an unnatural occurrence." Harriet grimaced and nodded her head in agreement.

"What puzzles me," Gideon said, concentration etched onto his face. "Is that Lord and Lady Macbeth had no children. So who is Lachlan?"

Harriet looked puzzled. "He referred to Lady Macbeth as 'mother'," she said, tilting her head as she pondered everything she could remember Lachlan saying.

"And we only know Lachlan's father as that, not as Lord Macbeth just now. Although, that must be who he is," Gideon continued.

"So…if Lord and Lady Macbeth had no children, how do they have one now?"

Harriet sat back as she pondered that question. A flash of insight came to her, as she remembered the trip to Verona. Caterina. Her existence could be the answer.

"When I went into Romeo and Juliet, there were…discrepancies," Harriet said, her mouth twisting. "I met Caterina, who wasn't in the original story." Harriet went on to explain how she had met Caterina, who she was and how she had featured in Romeo and Juliet's ending.

"So…she was able to change the ending of the story?" Gideon confirmed, blowing out a breath as Harriet nodded her head. "So, the story is fluid and you're able to influence and change it?" he asked.

"It seems that way," Harriet replied. Gideon looked impressed and terrified at the same time.

"I wonder how that works with the butterfly effect," Gideon murmured. But Harriet wasn't listening. A thought had struck her like lightning. She fumbled in the cloak she was still wearing for the book. Flipping through the pages nimbly, she paused as she reached Romeo and Juliet's entry. There, in bold black letters, was the name Caterina. Harriet breathed in sharply, her mind trying to fit the parts together to make a whole. If these names were in Shakespeare's notes, or what appeared to be his notes, how did they drop out of the stories?

"See, here," Harriet said, excitedly moving over to show Gideon the entry. Their shoulders brushed and she moved back self-consciously. "Caterina is listed in these notes, but she's nowhere in the final story. It's the same with Lachlan. Perhaps…perhaps the same thing happened to him?"

"Maybe," Gideon picked up the baton. "These are the characters who hold the key to changing the stories? You said Caterina was the catalyst for changing Juliet's ending. Perhaps Lachlan is the key to changing Macbeth's ending. It's undoubtedly a grisly one." Gideon grimaced.

"I hope not, for our sakes," Harriet said, a frown on her face. "Lachlan has been less than helpful so far, unlike the way Cat was."

"So we know where we are, and we've identified the character that doesn't fit again, thanks to the book. What we don't know is how or why we're here. Is there a reason we're here, or is it just chance?"

"I think you coming back with me was a mistake," Harriet said slowly. Gideon looked affronted, until she rushed to explain. "I mean,

I don't think you were supposed to travel. You were holding onto my leg when we resurfaced, and perhaps that pulled you through with me? I've been looking into Shakespeare's family tree…I was working on it when we left our time. It looks as though there might be a connection somewhere back in our family trees, somewhere where we overlap. But then, who knows? It's an online program, and there could be mistakes in it."

"Can either of your brothers travel?" Gideon asked.

"No," Harriet said slowly. "But then, I've not told them I can time shift either. I'm not even sure I have any control over moving through time myself. I certainly wasn't intending to do that when we were in the Derwent. Nevertheless, I don't think so. They wouldn't have been able to keep that a secret."

"Hmm," Gideon mused. "That's something to think about." A huge yawn split Gideon's face, and one followed on Harriet's moments later.

"Stop that," she said with a sigh. "It's contagious." Gideon grinned, then sobered quickly.

"I suggest that we get whatever sleep we can," he said, standing up from the bed and crossing to the chair. "It's late, and who knows what we'll have to do tomorrow. We'll think more clearly if we've slept." Harriet agreed, and she checked to see that Gideon was settling himself in the chair before she took her cloak off. She was still fully dressed, and so she felt a little silly being so shy about removing her cloak in front of Gideon. Harriet rushed to pull back the covers and slide into the bed, turning her back to Gideon and settling her head on the pillow. She could hear him settling down to sleep over in the corner.

Closing her eyes tightly, Harriet willed herself to sleep. She thought there was little chance she would get a moment's rest with Gideon so close in the same room, but she slid effortlessly into a deep, dreamless sleep within moments.

Chapter 9

Harriet woke with a start, to the feeling of light breathing on her face. Opening her eyes, they flew wide as she realised Gideon's face was mere centimetres from her own. Panic flooded through her as she moved rapidly backwards, falling out of the bed with an ungainly thump. She held her breath as Gideon stirred, then let it out at he settled back into sleep.

Heavy sleeper, Harriet thought as she crossed to the chair Gideon had vacated at some stage during the night. Settling in it, she couldn't blame him. It was as hard and unforgiving as the stone walls.

Harriet watched through the thin slit cut into the grey walls as the sun slid over the horizon and touched the hills and valleys surrounding Dunsinane, inch by inch. The calm of the early morning was unbroken: the birds hadn't even begun to chirp their waking songs.

Harriet hugged her knees and glanced over to the bed, where Gideon lay dead asleep. His black hair contrasted sharply with the linen pillows, and his handsome face was relaxed in sleep. He let out a tiny snore as he lay on his back, and Harriet smirked slightly.

Harriet turned back to her view of the outside world, narrow as it was. The countryside was as green as an emerald bed scattered with handfuls of amethysts: lush, rich and sparkling as far as the eye could see. Grey clouds scudded over the hills, shadowing the land as they passed in a swirling medley of monochrome. It was much more beautiful than Harriet's memories of travelling through it, as uncertain and gruelling as those hours had been.

Gradually, Harriet became aware of a thudding sound, growing louder and louder as the minutes ticked past. Peering awkwardly through the slitted wall, Harriet tried to find the source of the noise. It was the sound of a galloping horse…she had enough cause to know from their flight through the countryside a day earlier. Before long, Harriet saw a rider in the distance. He was racing hard, riding hell for leather, as her father would say. Harriet felt a pang as she remembered her father, and how far away he felt just now.

The rider approached the gates to Dunsinane, and the guard came to life on the other side of it. He spoke with the horseman briefly via the grate that had given them their first glimpse of Lord Macbeth the day prior. The guard jumped back, alarmed, and grabbed for a rope beside his guard post. Bells began to peal, clanging and ringing from the utmost towers of the castle.

Gideon sat bolt upright in bed, disoriented and alarmed. Couldn't quite sleep through that much noise, then. Harriet remained glued to the window, watching the events unfolding in the beaten earth courtyard below.

Pandemonium was the best way to describe it. Men were running, women were pulling layers of clothing on over the top of the ones they were already wearing. Sleep was being rubbed from eyes, and those who had overindulged the night before were stumbling up from where they had fallen, their eyes bloodshot and their steps shaky. A commanding voice cut through the hubbub of the crowd behind the gate. From Harriet's position, it was strange to see the milling crowd inside the gate and the single rider outside, the cause of all the commotion and calamity, yet unseen to all within the keep.

"Calm yeselves!" King Duncan's commanding tone rang through the courtyard, and silence fell. "What's the meaning of all this?"

"Banquo has come," the guard at the gate murmured, falling to his knees in deference before King Duncan.

"Why is he still outside the gate?" Macbeth materialised behind King Duncan. His face set in harsh lines, and he strode over to open the gate himself. The guard moved away from the chains that drew back the creaking, heavy timber gate.

"Why have ye ordered the ringing of the bells?" King Duncan asked as the gate creaked open heavily.

"My Lord," the guard said nervously. "Banquo brings news from Inverness and Moray. There has been an uprising. Yer sons have gone into hiding." The stunned crowd was silent for a long moment, before all hell broke loose. Harriet could feel Gideon behind her, trying to see into the courtyard, as Harriet was. Through the corner of her eye, the sparkling dark head of Lady Macbeth hove into view at the corner of the crowd. She stood at the top of the entrance stairs to the great hall, watching her husband greet his friend and hear Banquo's terrible news firsthand. Unperturbed, she surveyed the scene before her, then turned and glided back into the castle. Harriet watched her go, unsettled by her lack of reaction to the news that her home had been invaded.

Strange, Harriet pondered. They needed to sit down and revisit what Gideon could remember of Lady Macbeth. Perhaps she might play a more central role in this story than they had been expecting.

***

Dunsinane Castle was an eerie place in the wake of the news brought by Banquo. King Duncan was subdued. His men who had been placed at Inverness and Moray were marching back to the castle proper, but were days away yet. They had sent Banquo ahead to warn King Duncan that the crown of Scotland was in peril, and Macbeth that his lands were the site of the biggest uprising the country had seen. Duncan's sons, Malcolm and Donalbain, had fled the country.

In the wake of this distracting news, Harriet and Gideon found that they could traverse the castle with little interference. The only person who looked at them askance was Lachlan, but they did their best to remain out of his way. Even Aiden, the man who had ridden with Harriet behind him, had been amiable when he had seen them in the castle grounds.

They had missed breakfast, and by lunchtime their stomachs were aching with hunger. They needed to go down to the main hall to have any chance of finding food.

Lady Macbeth was the first person they saw as they entered the hall, and she waved them to a table not far from the main one. It would seem they were getting an upgrade from the servant's table.

Lady Macbeth seemed to favour red dresses: she had another on today that was as spectacular as the one she had worn the night before. She far outshone all of the other ladies present, of which there were only a handful. Beside her, Lord Macbeth's kilt-like attire matched the red of his wife's dress. They made a handsome pair – her so pale and slender, but with clouds of dark hair and piercing black eyes that were strangely iridescent. He was tall, broad shouldered and muscular, his face shadowed by a dark beard that matched his midnight hair. Both were greying, but that did little to diminish the latent power of the man. Lord Macbeth moved effortlessly, and it was clear to anyone who watched him for any length of time that he was military trained. A commander of troops, able to inspire loyalty in even the most recalcitrant of followers.

That could be a significant detail in the wake of the news from Banquo.

Gideon's memories of Macbeth's story, discussed during their morning together, had cast Lady Macbeth in a new light. Harriet had already viewed her warily, and they knew they were both strangely hypnotised by her presence. Shakespeare had apparently imbued her with voracious ambition, and he had given her a starring role in urging Macbeth to kill King Duncan.

Harriet shifted uneasily as she recalled the other details Gideon had remembered. He had recalled Banquo's death at the hands of Macbeth, who was supposed to be his closest friend and confidante. Gideon had explained that Macbeth and Banquo had heard the first prophecy together, and after the murder of Duncan, Macbeth is forced to kill Banquo so he cannot make the connection between Duncan's death and the prophecy. But something was off here. In the story Gideon knew, there was no uprising and no defeat of Duncan's troops. It was unholy murder, not a clash on the battlefield that had taken Duncan's life. Something wasn't connecting.

Sitting back, Harriet watched the castle's reaction to the news of the uprising. King Duncan had slid into his place at the main table, joining the Macbeths and his other guests. His face looked strained, and Harriet didn't miss the surreptitious glances he directed Lord Macbeth's way now and then. The man looked almost afraid, hunted even. Harriet frowned. That was a little unusual. She pondered what she knew. Macbeth lived in Inverness, and Lachlan was in training here in Dunsinane with Duncan, as per the Scottish tradition. Presumably that also explained Aiden's presence – the two were clearly close friends. Lord and Lady Macbeth had travelled to see King Duncan about the unrest in their lands, which had now turned into a full blown uprising in their absence. Duncan's men, including his sons, had been stationed in that part of Scotland to stop such an event from occurring, but the backlash from the locals and retainers of the northern lords had been powerful enough to send the sons of a King into exile.

I suppose it isn't that surprising that Duncan looks at Macbeth askance, Harriet thought as she ate what appeared to be stew. It's his lands and his people who are rebelling, against Duncan's rule presumably. But they didn't really know why the uprising had occurred, and Harriet resolved to find out before the day ticked over into a new one. She was aware of the urge to act, like an invisible clock was ticking somewhere and only she could hear it. Harriet was sure time was running out for someone, but she didn't know if it was Duncan, Banquo or someone else entirely.

Harriet glanced up at the head table to see Lachlan frowning down at her. His scowl had been retired, and it was the first time she had been his face without it. He was quite handsome, now that he wasn't trying to kidnap and ransom her. Still, he wasn't exactly her type. That position was held by the young man sitting next to her. Harriet still couldn't quite believe that he had taken this all in his stride so well. Imagine being told that you had travelled, what…900 years back in time? They had figured that out this morning, based on what Gideon could remember of the context around Macbeth's story. He had a very sharp mind and an even better memory, which just made him even more attractive to Harriet. She was going to be in very deep trouble if they remained together in this time for much longer. Perhaps that was the ticking she was hearing.

Harriet shook her head. Her mind had been ambling around in circles.

"Lachlan is coming this way," Gideon murmured, low enough so that the sound reached only Harriet's ears. Harriet looked up as Lachlan slid into the seat across from her on the long bench. He scrutinised them both as he cradled his mug of ale in his hands.

"So what…yer just decided to up and run off then?" Lachlan asked, taking a swig of his drink. Harriet eyed him, then inclined her head. She didn't speak, and Gideon took her lead.

"Tisn't that rather dangerous?" Lachlan asked, his interest clearly piqued.

Harriet shook her head. "It's more dangerous to stay where we were. Our families are locked in a blood feud, and if they knew that we planned to marry, who knows what would have happened."

Lachlan looked intrigued. Harriet wanted to divert the conversation away from them, before the questions became too pointed.

"Don't you have a…sweetheart of your own?" Harriet asked, studying Lachlan's face. He coloured slightly. Point scored, diversion success.

"Nay," he answered. "I've not got time fer that sort of thing. I'm in trainin' to the King o' Scotland," he said proudly. "Ain't got time fer marrying nobody."

"Well then, it's hard to explain," Harriet said, her tone conveying that the conversation about their elopement was at an end. "Perhaps one day you will find someone who changes that."

"Perhaps," Lachlan murmured, his eyes on his ale. He looked up again. "So what is it yer plan to do now?"

"You mean, now that we're not being ransomed?" Harriet said, a slight note of sarcasm sneaking into her tone. She felt confident enough that Lord and Lady Macbeth would not allow such a thing to happen, at least not at Lachlan's bidding. He seemed to be well under their control.

"Aye," Lachlan inclined his head. "My apologies fer that. Ye can never be too careful just now." Harriet inclined her head slightly.

"I suppose that we will wait until it is safe to travel," Harriet began.

"Ach, but ye cannae deprive us of yer wedding!" Lachlan exclaimed. Harriet felt Gideon's sharp intake of breath beside her and ruthlessly held the composure in her face.

"Say again?" Harriet said, frowning.

"Ye must have yer wedding here!" Lachlan exclaimed. Harriet eyed him suspiciously. What was his angle? There had to be one. In her limited experience, men didn't seem to care overly for weddings, or the details of them. What was Lachlan trying to pull?

"I mean, if that were yer purpose fer coming to Scotland, the least we can do is ter give yer what yer came for," Lachlan said, his eyes showing mischief and a little…malice? Perhaps he was testing them, after all. "If of course, that tis what yer came for?" Definitely testing.

"Of course we did," Gideon said indignantly.

"Well then," Lachlan said merrily. "I'll tell me mother yer happy ter get married here, at the castle." He stood up, and in doing so he missed the look of horror flit across Harriet and Gideon's faces. They had wiped the expressions off by the time he was ready to take his leave.

"Yer two will take some of the heat off me," Lachlan said, his tone convivial. "Mama will not be as interested in hounding me if she has yer wedding to take care of." With a slightly evil smirk, Lachlan bounded back to the head table and put his dark head close to his mother's. Both a diversion and a test then.

Harriet looked at Gideon in horror. "Oh no," she murmured. Gideon looked a little white. Before Lady Macbeth could waylay them, Harriet stood from her seat and gestured for Gideon to follow. He rose, zombie-like.

"We'll go back to the room," Harriet hissed, for his ears only. "We need to avoid Lady

MacWedding for as long as possible – at least until we figure out a solution to this problem."

Towing a pale Gideon behind her, Harriet exited the hall and made for the stone staircase that would carry them to their room. She slammed the door shut behind them. The echo reverberated down the hallway they had just left.

"Huh," Gideon grunted. It was the first noise he'd made since Lachlan had spoken to them. "Never thought I'd be married at 16. Is that even legal?"

"It is here," Harriet said grimly. Then she stopped and paused. "Well it is…if you're from here. But we're not! Gideon, this is great!"

"Speak for yourself," he murmured, his knees going out from under him as he slumped onto the bed.

"No listen," Harriet insisted. "Even if they do marry us here, it isn't legal. We're not bound in any way, even though they might go through the motions. But what it will do is allow me to get close to Lady Macbeth, and you to get closer to the men! I can find out information I wouldn't otherwise be able to, and you can keep an ear out for changes in the situation. They won't talk to me about uprisings, or wars or fights. But they'll talk to you. And Lady Macbeth will speak to me about her home, her family and her observations. I would be willing to bet that they're sharper than anyone else knows."

"But…Lady Macbeth is somewhat of a sociopath, according to Shakespeare's version," Gideon said. Despite Harriet's rising excitement, he clearly had reservations. "What if she does something to you? Or comes to suspect something, especially if you're getting closer to her?"

"You have to trust me," Harriet said, her eyes beseeching Gideon to have faith in her. "And I have to believe in you. We each have a role to play, and if we do that right, maybe we'll find what we're meant to do here and we can go home."

Gideon sighed. "I suppose it's the best plan we have right now."

"It is," Harriet said firmly. Then she smiled intently. "If Lady Macbeth wants a wedding, she'll get a wedding."

Gideon gulped, audibly.

Chapter Ten

Having something to do, something to actively work towards, helped Harriet to move in what she thought was the right direction. As much as her stomach fluttered at the thought of going through with a fake wedding to Gideon, she was hoping that they would be able to defuse the situation and return home before it became a real problem.

Mid-afternoon saw Harriet and Gideon sitting in the keep of the castle, in plain view of anyone and everyone. They were waiting to see what would happen next – making themselves available to anyone who wished to approach them.

Although Dunsinane Castle wasn't the largest – as far as castles go, anyway – there was plenty to see. Especially for two people who lived 900 years into the future. The Scottish summer days seemed to stretch forever, with the gap between day and night extending for hours. Everything they could see was packed in behind the stone walls of the keep. The baker, the butcher, the blacksmiths, the stables – all that the people of the castle needed was right here.

From their perch on the top of their hill, they could see for miles and miles around. Their view was only impeded by Birnam Wood, its dense trees marching away as far as the eye could see. Even so, anyone approaching the castle, from any angle, would be clearly visible for miles before they could reach the big wooden gates protecting the castle's inhabitants.

Plenty of people exchanged greetings with them as they sat in the weak afternoon sunlight, Harriet swinging her legs as she perched atop the stone half-wall dividing the main keep from the stables and workshop areas. Gideon stood beside her, casually leaning against the wall.

"How long do you think it will be before one of them turns up?" Gideon asked out of the side of his mouth.

"It's just a hunch," Harriet said, smiling as she spoke, just in case they were being watched. "But I don't think Lady Macbeth is all she seems. Surely it was her who got us out of that prison – why? What was in it for her? There has to be something. We're pretty sure that Lachlan's motivation is to avoid his mother matching him with some young woman, but Lady Macbeth's intentions are something else entirely. Your description of her in Shakespeare's version was disturbing."

Harriet lapsed into silence as Gideon nodded his head.

They didn't have long to wait. Lady Macbeth herself glided out of the castle doors and made straight for where they were seated not far away. Lachlan stalked in her wake.

"Harriet. Gideon. How are ye this fine day?" Lady Macbeth's manner was smooth and practised. She was clearly used to people falling in line with her wishes.

"It is a lovely day," Harriet replied, diverting the lady's grand entrance by glancing up at the clear skies and prattling on. She took a little vindictive pleasure in unsettling Lady Macbeth's plans – she could see that Lady Macbeth was waiting with increasing impatience for her incessant chatter to cease. Still…she was an important source of information, and it was crucial that they not alienate her either.

"Lachlan tells me that yer wish to have yer wedding here!" Lady Macbeth said brightly.

Harriet slanted a sideways glance at Lachlan. He was smiling innocently. Wish to indeed!

Turning her attention back to Lady Macbeth, Harriet made agreeable noises. Before long, Lady Macbeth had Harriet walking back inside the castle while Lachlan steered Gideon towards the stables. Harriet glanced back over her shoulder, just as Gideon looked back for her. Harriet smiled a little shyly, and allowed Lady Macbeth to steer her into the gloom of the castle interior.

Harriet followed Lady Macbeth over the flagstones of the entry way, grey and forbidding despite the sunshine outside. Not a great deal of the outside penetrated the inside, and Harriet now understood the chill that pervaded their room after nightfall. Lady Macbeth strode through the castle as if it were indeed her own, although Harriet knew it wasn't. But come to think of it, she hadn't seen King Duncan's wife, the Queen, while she had been there. She wondered if that was because there wasn't a Queen. It would seem difficult for Lady Macbeth to walk around as if she owned the place if there were a Queen in residence.

Harriet mentally shook herself as Lady Macbeth steered her into her sitting room. The familiar room was relatively soothing, which was helpful given Harriet's nerves at being left alone with the imposing lady. The fact that she was hoping to shape their interaction to suit her own purposes didn't make the icily beautiful lady any less intimidating. She had to concentrate and not fall under Lady Macbeth's spell, as she seemed to be prone to do.

"Och, Harriet," Lady Macbeth waved a slender hand. "Have a seat and make yerself comfortable." She sank down onto the chair nearest the fireplace: the twin of the one Harriet was about to sit in. Lady Macbeth's rich red skirts rustled as she shifted slightly, and the jewels embroidered into her gown winked in the firelight that seemed to burn all day despite the season. Summer in Scotland was still cold, especially inside the castle.

"So," Lady Macbeth's obsidian eyes glittered as they focused on Harriet's hazel ones. "We've a wedding to plan, no?"

Harriet didn't think she was being offered a way out. It was more of a rhetorical question, and she took it as such.

"Yes," Harriet answered brightly. Then she let her face fall a little, as if she had remembered something that was troubling her. "But…we were wondering. We're so far from home, and we know nothing about your country or where we are. Perhaps you could tell me a little about Scotland…to help my nerves." Harriet smiled winningly. Lady Macbeth regarded her through narrowed eyes, but Harriet held her nerve. Perhaps she had overplayed it a little. Lady Macbeth settled into her seat more fully. "Well then…I suppose that makes sense. What is it ye wish to know?"

Before she fully formulated a plan, or thought out what she was going to say, Harriet found herself telling Lady Macbeth, quite genuinely, how much she missed her own mother. Weddings were a time for families, and a special time between mother and daughter in particular. She talked about the sorrow she felt at being separated from her family, although she had chosen the separation to be with Gideon. Harriet could see that something in Lady Macbeth was responding to what she was saying – perhaps she had been separated from her own mother as well?

But the more Harriet talked, the more she could see that something wasn't quite right with Lady Macbeth. At times her face softened, and she seemed like a kind-hearted, motherly figure. Then her face would harden unexpectedly, her eyes would glitter almost forcefully and her words became harsher. It was almost like having a conversation with two people, or more accurately, two personalities. It was perplexing. As Harriet watched, it was almost as though two women were forcing their way to the surface of Lady Macbeth – one kind and welcoming, the other calculating and cold.

Harriet's approach changed, and she tried to spin out her time with the kind-hearted Lady Macbeth for as long as she could. She avoided digging for information, instead allowing Lady Macbeth to speak as she wished. It was against Harriet's natural inclination to sit back and do nothing, to say nothing, but she found that her own mother's strategy of saying little was paying off in this situation. Usually, Carolyn Hunter used it to get information out of her children, but it seemed to be effective here too.

"And so we visit Dunsinane regularly. Probably more so than 'tis usual, but I do so miss my Lachlan when we're up in the wilds o' Inverness, and he is down here with the King." Lady Macbeth stared into the fire as she talked, her face soft in repose.

Harriet made sympathetic noises. "Is there no Queen here at Dunsinane?" Harriet asked, trying to sound innocent.

"Oh no child, there hasnae been fer some time," Lady Macbeth answered. It didn't seem that she wanted to elaborate further on that.

"King Duncan has been the King of Scotland for many years."

"Lady Macbeth…"

"Och please, call me Gruoch." It was the kind Lady Macbeth who spoke as she said it.

Harriet tried the strange name on her own tongue and found it as difficult to say as she had anticipated. Gruoch smiled slightly, as though she knew of Harriet's difficulty. She made no move to take back her decree, though.

"Gruoch," Harriet continued, the name still sounding a little off in her accent. "You said that you came to Dunsinane to speak with King Duncan?"

"Aye" Gruoch sighed heavily. "He was meant to be in Inverness, visiting oor castle. But we rode south to warn him of the unrest up in oor lands before he got close to the fighting."

"Why are they fighting?" Harriet asked. Her genuine curiosity was evident.

Gruoch sighed again. "There are men in the north who believe that my husband should be the rightful heir ter the Scottish crown," Gruoch explained. "King of Alba, as Duncan's official title says. Duncan's sons, Malcolm and Donalbain, are next in line through their father, of course, but some say they aren't fit ter rule. Both are young and inexperienced in the ways of oor country...," Gruoch trailed off, her eyes focusing sharply. Harriet recognised the change and took a swift step back from the line of questioning. "Of course, we dinnae believe that at all," Gruoch said rather stiffly. "We will always support oor King Duncan."

Harriet was perplexed. This was the weirdest conversation she'd ever been a part of, and that included the many unexpected twists and turns she had on her last trip back into Shakespeare's stories.

That seemed to be all that Grouch wished to speak of in relation to herself or her family. She swiftly brought the conversation back to Harriet and Gideon marrying, and Harriet sighed a little inside as she hoped Gideon was having better luck with Lachlan and the other men.

***

Gideon had indeed had fared well with Lachlan, and it seemed with his father, Lord Macbeth. Harriet was yet to meet the man, and she listened to Gideon's recount of his afternoon from her perch in the middle of the lumpy mattress with growing resentment. She had spent the afternoon talking about dresses, rings and flowers, while Gideon had been getting his hands dirty with the real stuff. Harriet blew out a frustrated breath.

"And they talked about their allegiance to King Duncan…it seemed genuine," Gideon finished, waving his hands as he spoke.

"Lady Macbeth – Gruoch as I'm to call her – was the same," Harriet said, propping her chin on her hand. "Although, it was by far the strangest conversation I've ever been part of." Harriet told Gideon of her afternoon, including the plans that they had made so far for their pending nuptials.

"They've set the wedding for one week from today, so that's our deadline. Unless you fancy getting hitched," Harriet grinned cheekily. Gideon smiled back tentatively. It seemed he didn't really know what to say, so he said nothing. Smart boy.

"Gruoch seemed preoccupied…not with the wedding plans though. They appear to be almost a distraction to her – who knows why she even wants to do this." Harriet waved her hands in exasperation. Then her face lit up as a thought occurred to her. "I've got it," she breathed. "Gruoch doesn't want to be distracted – she wants to provide a distraction. While everyone else is focusing on a wedding, it's hard to pay attention to much else. I think we're a smokescreen for something…but what?" Harriet frowned.

"Lachlan told me that we're to meet King Duncan this evening at dinner," Gideon said, his face contemplative. "We cannot marry without his permission, but both Lachlan and Macbeth didn't foresee any difficulties. As long as we stick with our story, we should be fine."

Harriet nodded. She looked down at her knees and plucked at the serviceable brown dress that she wore, given to her by the ladies in the forest. "I wish I had something else to change into. It's weird wearing the same thing, day in and day out."

"Ah!" Gideon exclaimed, just as a knock fell on their door. "But you won't have to." He didn't elaborate further, just crossed to the door and opened it. He murmured his thanks to whoever was there, and closed the door again. But as he turned, Harriet could see he had a forest green dress draped over his arms.

"Compliments of the King," Gideon said, holding up his arms ceremoniously. He cheekily bent down on one knee and presented the dress to Harriet, his head bowed. Harriet scrambled off the bed to take the heavy material from his arms, spreading the dress across the bed so she could see it better.

It wasn't as magnificent as the clothes in Juliet's time, but it was serviceable and beautiful. And it looked lovely and warm. The forest green material glowed in the twilight gloom permeating the room. Nestled along the front of the dress was a double strand of the most perfect pearls Harriet had ever seen. She gasped as she picked them up, holding them up to the fading light. They seemed to take on a life of their own, pulsing with vitality. As she set them down again, Harriet saw a simple headband, decorated with matching pearls, laying alongside the dress. It was a gorgeous ensemble.

Harriet looked at Gideon in amazement. "Is this really mine to wear?" she asked incredulously.

"Yes," Gideon smiled. "It's a gift from the King. Apparently it used to belong to his wife and has not been used in years. Lord Macbeth said that it was his wish that you put it to good use again."

"Lord Macbeth," Harriet said, her eyes searching Gideon's. "How…what?"

Gideon explained the connection. Macbeth had told Gideon of the dress, and relayed the King's wishes. He was busy on official business, but he had been told of the situation of the two young people staying in his castle and was eager to show his hospitality. It was even more of a turnaround from the way that Lachlan had initially treated them. Harriet had been half afraid that Duncan would also want to ransom them back to England when he met them, but it seemed that wasn't to be the case.

"There will be another on the day of our…wedding," Gideon said with a gulp. Harriet eyes laughed as they met his. It was amusing to watch him struggle with that element.

"So…what will you wear?" Harriet asked, looking around for another pile of clothes. Gideon smiled shyly.

"I'm going to leave you to change, and then collect you in about half an hour. Lachlan has some clothes for me to wear – we are close to the same size. I'm going to go and get those now." Gideon made for the door. He turned back to look at Harriet as he pulled it open.

"I'll see you shortly," he murmured, his eyes on her face. Harriet nodded – she knew her cheeks were flushed.

As the door closed softly, Harriet turned back to inspect her new dress. She had thirty minutes to make herself as beautiful as she could.

These would give her an excellent head start.

Chapter Eleven

A light tap on the door announced Gideon's return.

"Can I come in?" Harriet heard his voice float through the door. She called out for him to enter, and watched as the door swung wide and Gideon turned back to close it. She stared. Gideon turned around and stepped into the room, but stopped swiftly in his tracks. He stared too.

Harriet was a vision in green – the soft, woollen material of the dress sat well on her and the cut suited her figure. The pearls around her neck glowed in the firelight, as did those sitting atop her fiery red hair. She had swept it back and up, in much the same way that she had seen Gruoch do, and it sat softly off her face, anchored by the pearl band.

Gideon seemed to be having trouble getting his breath back, and Harriet couldn't blame him. She was suffering from the same affliction.

He looked completely different as well. Gone were the clothes of an itinerant traveller – albeit a moderately well-to-do one. In its place was what looked like woollen leggings, covered with a dark grey tunic cinched at the waist with a leather belt. Over the top of this sat a leather jacket without sleeves, its panels crossing Gideon's chest diagonally. With his dark hair and clear complexion, he had never looked more handsome to Harriet. She shook her head and tried to get her wits back.

"Ahh…" she said, searching desperately for something to say. "Um." Clearly, the words weren't there to be found. Gideon said nothing, just stood in place, dumbstruck.

Voices floated up to them from the courtyard of the keep below. They were low and urgent, and they pierced through the spell weaving its way around Harriet and Gideon. She blinked and focused her attention on their words.

"But we must, my Lord." It was a woman's voice, hushed but strangely familiar. Gruoch. Harriet recognised it, as a shiver she didn't understand slid down the nape of her neck. Putting her finger to her lips, she moved almost soundlessly to cross to the slit in their stone walls. Gideon prowled in her wake.

"I cannae do that, my love," came a voice that Harriet couldn't place. She frowned.

"Lord Macbeth," Gideon breathed in her ear.
"I cannae betray my friend – my Lord," Macbeth said again.
"Ye must summon the spirits again this night," Gruoch commanded, her voice hard and clear. Gideon looked perplexed, but he hadn't seen Gruoch in action earlier that day. This was the malignant side of Gruoch – the woman Harriet had glimpsed during the afternoon.
"Midnight tonight," Gruoch said. "Then we will see what we see." The sound of swishing material and light footsteps filtered up to them through the crevice in the stone. Measured, heavier footsteps followed after, slower and more ponderous than Gruoch's had been.
Harriet turned to Gideon, her eyes wide. His face was inches was from hers. He stepped back quickly, and Harriet rapped her head sharply on the stone as she jerked her away. It might have been funny if she wasn't so affected by it.
It wasn't long before she was pacing the room, kicking her skirts out of her way as she turned at the end of each length.
"Tell me again everything you know about the story of Macbeth," Harriet demanded. Gideon sat down in the chair by the fire, turning to face her as she wore a track in the floor. He

patiently steeped his fingers and consulted his memory.

"Macbeth is Duncan's man. He controls Inverness and the northern territories, alongside other Lords. He is also related to Duncan somehow in the original play – because when Duncan is murdered he inherits the power of the crown."

"Despite the fact that Duncan has two sons?" Harriet asked, pausing in her pacing to look at Gideon. He inclined his head in agreement. Harriet resumed striding across the room and back.

"Macbeth receives a prophecy from three witches that he is to be King of Scotland. They encounter Macbeth and Banquo as they ride from the battlefield – I can't remember where or why." He frowned in concentration. "The sisters make three prophecies: the first two regarding Macbeth, and the last for Banquo. They say that Macbeth shall be named as Thane of Cawdor and then king. Banquo, although he shall not rule Scotland himself, will be father to future generations of kings." Gideon trailed off, retreating into his memory as he tried to recall further details. Harriet made a sound of frustration.

"Yes, yes, I remember that," she said impatiently. "But it's a prophecy. That's like a fortune teller back in our time."

"That's true," Gideon agreed. "But it isn't so much about what is prophesised, rather, it is what Macbeth and his wife do about it. Just like in our own time. Lady Macbeth convinces her husband to murder Duncan while he is visiting them in Inverness. He then seizes the crown of Scotland and disinherits Duncan's sons. But Banquo also heard the prophecy, and Lady Macbeth decrees that they must murder Macbeth's closest friend to ensure that he cannot speak against them. Banquo comes back to haunt the Macbeths, and her guilt drives Lady Macbeth mad. She eventually dies. Macbeth is killed in battle by Malcolm, Duncan's son, who is backed by the English." He shook his head. "I don't remember much more than that, unfortunately."

"It's much more than I'd know without you," Harriet said, her pacing abated for the moment. She studied Gideon, sitting in the hard chair before the fire.

"We must go down to dinner. King Duncan is expecting to meet us," Gideon said, pushing up from the seat.

"Perhaps we will find out more tonight," Harriet mused. "And at midnight…we will be watching Gruoch and Macbeth, one way or another."

***

Harriet could feel hundreds of pairs of eyes on her as she walked into the cavernous dining hall. Conversation seemed to stop momentarily, then start up again as Gideon led Harriet to the head table, as he had been instructed to do.

Lachlan saw them approaching and rose from his seat, gesturing for them to sit to his left. There were two empty chairs that hadn't been there the night before, clearly intended for Harriet and Gideon.

This close to the head table, Harriet could see the old, beautifully jewelled and carved King and Queen chairs, positioned so proudly at the centre of the long table. The King occupied his chair, but the one beside him had been empty since their arrival in this time.

"Allow me to introduce ye to my father," Lachlan said to Harriet, waving towards Lord Macbeth.

"Welcome," Macbeth said, his voice low and gravelly. This was the first time Harriet had actually heard him speak in a proper conversation, without his voice raised in command or in hushed tones she wasn't supposed to hear.

"I trust that ye are keeping well," he said politely, seating himself again as Harriet took her place. He had risen alongside his son as Harriet and Gideon had approached.

"I am, my Lord," Harriet replied, inclining her head as a maid popped up from nowhere to place dishes of food closer to her setting. Harriet recoiled slightly as the maid took the lid off one pot and she saw the boiled meat inside. Her palate, or her stomach, wasn't used to so much meat, and it seemed there were many different ways to eat the various animals perched in front of the most important lords and ladies at the table.

Macbeth had finished his first course and was sipping from a golden goblet with a stunning, raw sapphire set into the dull glint of the beaten metal. Gruoch had risen from her chair and come to stand behind Harriet's.

"Ye must make yer curtesy to the King," Gruoch hissed in Harriet's ear as she rounded the end of the head table. Harriet bobbed up obediently as if she were a puppet, unable to control her own actions. She followed Gruoch to stand in front of the giant table. Gideon hastily joined them.

"Yer Majesty," Gruoch said, curtseying low. Harriet followed suit. "Allow me ter introduce Lady Harriet Hunter and Lord Gideon White, who are visiting us from near to England."

The King set down his goblet, embellished with even more magnificent jewels than the one held by Macbeth. His golden eyes skewered Harriet, as if he could see straight through her and the cover story they had concocted. Harriet steeled her nerves and tried not to flinch – they couldn't be exposed now.

"Ter be married, I hear," Duncan mused, studying the pair. Harriet nodded politely, keeping her head down and mirroring Gruoch's moves. She could feel Gideon bowing low beside her. The King waved his hand and Gruoch rose from her deep curtesy to stand straight and tall in front of her ruler. Again, Harriet followed, her heart thudding in her ears.

"What is it like? Where ye hail from?" King Duncan asked Harriet, interest gleaming in his eyes.

"It is much the same as here," Harriet said evasively. "We have a monarchy and we are expected to follow the rules."

"Ach," Duncan said, sitting back in his chair and resting his head against the jewelled back of the imposing throne. "Rules are something oor people do not know much about these days."

Harriet looked at the King inquiringly but chose to remain silent.

"Ye will have heard o' the rebels around these parts and further north." Duncan continued, picking up his goblet again. Harriet could see that Macbeth kept his face studiously blank.

Harriet nodded. "I had heard there has been some trouble. I understand that's why we cannot travel on." Harriet's voice sounded steady, but inside her heart was racing like a thoroughbred's after a major race.

"Ach," Duncan said, his head dropping sadly. "Oor land tis not safe fer a young couple such as yerselves just now. Lord, tis not even safe for meself. But that will change." Duncan's face grew darker as he thought about the uprisings against his own rule.

With a few murmured words, Macbeth diverted his King's attention. Gruoch gestured for them to sit and seated herself at the table once more. Harriet blew out a breath. That had been more nerve-racking than being close to Gideon.

Seated between Lachlan and Gideon, Harriet had the opportunity to speak with both men, and to enjoy their conversation as it flowed over her head. She also had a unique opportunity to observe the hall before her, as the tables spilled out in long lines of mostly men breaking bread with one another. The atmosphere in the great hall wasn't the same this evening as it had been the night before. News of the unrest in Macbeth's own lands had cast a pall over the assembled company, and many held their conversations in hushed tones. More than once Harriet saw a worried glance directed at Macbeth or King Duncan, and no one seemed to be partaking in the ale with quite as much abandonment as they had the evening before. It was a subdued feast, and if that was clear to Harriet, she assumed it hadn't gone unnoticed by the others at the head table either.

In fact, King Duncan seemed to break from the dining table quite early – the surprise on Macbeth's face showed his retreat from the feasting hall at this hour was unusual. The lord had carefully controlled his features after the immediate tell-tale signs – he was clearly a well-practiced politician. Gruoch seemed unperturbed, but then little seemed to ruffle her feathers.

As Macbeth and Gruoch took their leave of the assembled company, Harriet and Gideon took the opportunity to do the same. Lachlan joined some other young men, one of who

Harriet recognised as Aiden, at a nearby table. He seemed content enough.

Harriet and Gideon hurried up the circular stairs to their room, closing the door silently behind them.

"What time is it?" Harriet hissed as soon as they were inside.

"It can't be later than 10pm," Gideon answered, looking at what they could see of the outside world. "Though these long summers make it hard to be sure."

"We need to find out where Macbeth will be tonight at midnight, and make sure we're there," Harriet whispered, overly cautious in her trepidation and excitement. Finally, they were making some sort of meaningful progress.

Frustration had ridden Harriet hard in the afternoon hours that she'd been forced to while away, planning an event that would hopefully never happen with Gruoch. She was ready for action, to take matters into her hands and change whatever it was that they were here to change. Unlike in Juliet's story, Harriet had no clue what they were supposed to do here. Were they meant to stop Macbeth from killing his King? That seemed unlikely, as they were at Dunsinane and not Macbeth's Inverness Castle. The setting was wrong. Was this something to do with Lachlan, a character who mimicked Caterina from Verona – neither had been in the final Shakespearean story, but both appeared in his book of notes. Or was it something else entirely.

Harriet sighed as she sank onto the edge of the bed, her mind awash with confusion and half-formed ideas.

Macbeth's little midnight sojourn had better yield something they could work with.

Chapter Twelve

Harriet crept into the courtyard, the weak moonlight glinting off the pearls in her hair. She drifted like a wraith to the low wall she'd been sitting on that afternoon, hoping that it might offer her a good vantage point for whatever Macbeth was planning. She had left Gideon sleeping in the room – he'd fallen into a deep sleep as she had sat, peering out of their tiny view on the world. Harriet had watched the stars swirl in the deep blue sky as she organised her thoughts.

She'd never seen any sort of magic – of course she hadn't, it didn't exist. Unless you counted what she could do, but somewhere deep down, Harriet knew that she couldn't personally control how or when she travelled through time. It seemed to happen to her, rather than be influenced by her. It wasn't magical.

But what Macbeth was about to do sure sounded like it might qualify. Summoning spirits was something Harriet had only ever seen done in movies, or talked about at cheesy girls' nights. Harriet crouched down behind the half-wall, her skirts trailing on the hard packed dirt. Without a watch or clock, it was impossible to tell what time it was. But she was confident she hadn't missed Macbeth – she had been watching out for him since they had returned from dining in the hall. Unless he had snuck past her during her fleet-footed trip down the darkened halls to the side door she had spotted that afternoon, he was yet to appear.

The mist that was a part of Scotland reached even inside the castle keep. It crept along the ground, wreathing Harriet's ankles.

Her ears pricked up at the sound of a door grating open – the same door that she had exited from not long before. Letting out a small breath, Harriet thanked heaven for small mercies that she hadn't been slightly later, or that she hadn't waited for Gideon to wake. The sound of low voices reached her across the courtyard, the volume increasing as they walked closer to her hiding place. It was definitely the man she'd been waiting for. His low, measured tones were easy to pick out. And so were Lady Macbeth's.

"The spirits last appeared to yer on the moors," Gruoch said, her voice hushed. "And ye did nothing to summon them. But yer need to try, if ye don't believe the message they've already given yer. Go outside the walls of the castle, like we talked about. If they know ye are looking for them, they'll find ye." Gruoch ushered her husband to the side of the castle keep, a mere ten metres from where Harriet crouched, holding her breath. She couldn't afford for either of them to see her now.

Lord Macbeth pushed a stone into the wall and a small opening appeared in the strong, fortified walls. Harriet's mouth dropped open. She had been expecting him to open the huge, creaking front gate, and was wondering how on earth he would accomplish it at midnight without waking the guards or anyone else within the castle proper. It didn't exactly have quiet hinges.

Harriet watched as Macbeth slipped outside and Gruoch pushed another stone to shut the door. It was a genius contraption, really. Harriet mentally shook herself and concentrated on watching, while not being seen herself. She could hear Macbeth's footsteps outside the stone walls – it sounded as though he was sticking close to the shelter and darkness their imposing height would provide. Harriet's attention was caught by a small spark of purple light that flickered to life not far from her hiding place. Then she heard Gruoch's voice. Even though she could not have been five metres from the lady, her voice sounded like it was coming from a great distance. It took on a different tone – she sounded deeper, more self-assured and in command than she ever had.

"Sisters, I challenge thee to stop me," Gruoch intoned. Harriet's eyes flew wide. She sounded menacing, even a little evil. "Try as ye will to convince Macbeth he shouldnae follow this road of ruin. Ye willnae defeat me: ye willnae divert him from this course. His actions will avenge the wrongs done to me centuries ago. I willnae rest until Duncan and all of his kin pay fer their treachery. Try as ye will to stop me, 'twill fall on deaf ears." Gruoch's voice lapsed into silence, but Harriet could feel the power pulsing from her. The stone wall did nothing to stop the strong waves from washing around and through Harriet. In the silence left by Gruoch, Harriet focused on the lighter, more delicate voices that she could only just discern through the thick keep walls. She strained her ears – her only source of information with her sight obstructed. At the same time, she held her hand over her mouth to try and quiet her breathing. She felt as though Gruoch should have been able to hear her heart beating madly at such close proximity.

"We can only repeat the prophecy we have already given ye, my Lord," a tinkling voice was saying. It sounded vaguely familiar, but Harriet couldn't place it. "Ye will become Thane of Cawdor, and then King o' Scotland."

Macbeth murmured something, but Harriet couldn't hear it.

"Banquo will father the next line of Kings," another pretty voice said. "Ye do nae have a son ter inherit from ye."

Again, Macbeth's murmured voice halted the lighter voices, but again Harriet could not hear it properly.

"Ye will be safe on yer throne, until Birnam Wood comes ter Dunsinane. Ye cannot be killed by any man born of a woman." The first voice spoke again.

"Ye must choose yer own destiny, Macbeth," came a third voice. It was the antithesis of what Gruoch's tone had been. This voice radiated confidence as well, but it was soothing and comforting, not challenging and menacing. "We can nae, and must nae, choose fer yer. Only ye can determine what is right."

Harriet felt rather than saw a rush of power – whether it was from the weird Gruoch, who now frightened the life out of her, or from the voices outside she couldn't be sure. She listened as Gruoch pushed the stone to re-open the hole in the wall and Macbeth slipped back inside.

"Are ye convinced now, husband?" Gruoch asked, her voice having lost its other-worldly quality.

"I must do what is right," Macbeth replied. Harriet could see him shaking his dark head from her vantage point. She could also feel Gruoch's exasperation and impatience surge, but it was cloaked as quickly as it appeared.

"Of course ye must," Gruoch said, almost soothingly.

"I cannae kill my own King," Macbeth lamented, his voice shaking. Harriet watched as Gruoch pinched the bridge of her nose, unseen by her husband who was closing the secret entrance once more.

"We will decide together," Gruoch said, winding her arm through Macbeth's as he turned. Charm radiated around her as she walked with her husband, away from Harriet and towards the castle. "We will do what is best."

Harriet held her breath until they were in the castle, and then she remained where she was, despite her screaming muscles. She wasn't game to move until she knew they would be well inside and away from the door. Harriet knew no other way back in, other than the front door that would wake everyone who heard it creaking open. Besides, her mind was racing too much to move an inch.

There had been three voices outside – they had been distinct and separate, despite having the same qualities. And each was eerily familiar, but she couldn't place them. Gruoch's weirdo act was something else again. What had happened? Harriet knew that Lady Macbeth – Gruoch, whoever she was – seemed to have multiple sides to her personality. But what had that purple light been? Had that come from her? And who were her sisters? It seemed almost as though she had summoned the three outside…Harriet's eyes flew wide. Had she? But that seemed crazy.

Harriet shook her head. Why was she having so much trouble believing what was happening? Hell, she was in a time 900 years before her own, in another country, and she had taken Gideon back with her. Was it really that much of a stretch to have faith in what was happening here? Breathing deeply, Harriet stared up at the night sky. The view was so much clearer out here than when she had been trying to do the same thing through the slit in the stone wall. Cocking her head to the side, Harriet studied the pulsing blue star they had seen on their journey to Dunsinane Castle. It seemed to be in a different position, as if it had moved slightly since they had been in this time. Harriet shrugged and studied the rest of the sky. It was such a pretty sight, even if she was cramped and cold in a darkened corner of a medieval castle keep. But the stiffness in her legs was prompting her to move, and she thought about how long it had been since the Macbeths had headed inside. She should be safe by now.

Harriet crept out of the shadows, using the other darkened places around the keep to make her way back to the external door hidden into the side of the castle. On silent feet, she studied the door as she approached it. All was still and quiet, and she'd need to unlatch the door to get inside. Which was easy enough, but Harriet wouldn't know if there was anyone near the inside of the door until she was through it. Steeling herself, Harriet grasped the handle. And quickly let it go again as she felt pressure pushing against her hand, and heard the slight scream of steel on steel. Melting back into the shadows against the castle wall, Harriet winced as she watched the door open slowly. She hoped she was invisible in the dark. It was a man coming through the door, and Harriet breathed a sigh of relief as she recognised Gideon's broad shoulders. Ridiculously happy to see him, she popped up out of the shadows, a huge smile on her face. And almost gave him a heart attack. As he turned, Harriet instinctively clapped her hand over his mouth. She felt the tension in his body ease as he realised it was Harriet in front of him.

"Inside now," Harriet hissed in his ear. Letting him go, she slid through the doorway. He followed closely behind. Silently, they tiptoed back to the room, Harriet's heart jumping at every movement, every sound.

Shutting the door, she spun around with her back to it, breathing out a sigh of pure relief. Gideon stopped in the centre of the room.

"Where were you?" he demanded, his eyebrows knit together. "I woke up – though I don't remember going to sleep – and you were gone."

"I went down to the courtyard to see what Macbeth was planning."

"You what!" Gideon hissed, his eyebrows flying upwards. "Are you mad?"

Harriet frowned. "Actually, I learned quite a lot."

"That was insanely dangerous," Gideon declared, his voice rising. Harriet hushed him, her eye on the door.

"Don't shush me," Gideon said, his eyes flashing. "Macbeth is responsible for the murdering two people, including his best friend. What do you think he'd do to you if he found you wandering around?"

"It's his wife I'm more worried about," Harriet muttered, moving compulsively to check that the keep was still deserted. She had to tell Gideon what had happened, but she had the feeling she'd be struck down as soon as she tried. "And Macbeth is not Lachlan's father.

"What do you mean?" Gideon asked, frowning.

Harriet pushed him into the armchair in agitation and started pacing. She kept her voice low as she told Gideon everything she'd seen.

"But who is Lachlan's father? And the purple light makes no sense," Harriet finished, frowning.

"I don't have an answer for Lachlan," Gideon replied. "But the light actually does make sense. It was light that woke me up, but it wasn't purple. When I got to the window – or whatever it's called – I saw three streams of white light. I thought I was hallucinating, or still asleep, but they came up from just outside the castle walls and disappeared into the sky. We can't both be imagining things."

Harriet mulled that over as she sat on the edge of the bed, her gaze unfocused. She looked up at Gideon, sitting in the chair, studying her face.

"What do we do now?"

Chapter Thirteen

The next morning, they had their answer. A scream rent the air just before the sun snuck over the horizon. The castle burst into life as though lightning had struck it. Men ran around, hastily pulling on their boots as they criss-crossed each other in the courtyard below Harriet and Gideon's window. Harriet sat up, bleary-eyed after her late night encounter in the dark with Lord and Lady Macbeth, and the spirits they had summoned. Gideon jerked awake beside her, his dark eyes staring at the ceiling above their heads as his brain struggled to catch up with his body. Turning his head, he stared at Harriet. And he smiled.

It was a genuine smile, as brilliant and golden as the sun that was rising to scatter its rays through the Scottish countryside. Harriet blinked, completely disarmed. Any part of her that had been holding back, any little piece of her heart that she had hidden away to prevent its destruction, gave up the fight and surrendered to her feelings. She had loved Gideon since the second grade, when he had coaxed her down, terrified, from the top of the two storey jungle gym. Watching him grow into a mature, caring and quite frankly, beautiful, young man had done nothing to dull those feelings.

Eyes like stormy skies, Gideon studied her as she sat, frozen, clutching the sheets to her chest. His face was calm, serene even, and he arched an eyebrow at Harriet as if he knew her secret. Maybe he did.

A shout from outside brought Harriet back to the present, and she scrambled from the bed with her cheeks flaming scarlet. She'd try to deal with that later. Peeking through the long, slender hole in the wall, Harriet watched the bustle of activity in the courtyard below with a terrible sense of dejavu.

"Did you hear that scream?" Harriet cleared her throat as it cracked a little.

"Is that what that was?" Gideon asked, swinging his long legs down from the mattress. He stretched his back as he sat up fully on the edge of the bed.

"I think so." Harriet's reply was muffled as she squeezed her face as far as she could into their window on the world, trying to see as much as she possibly could. "I can't tell what's happening," she said in disgust, turning away from the stone wall.

"So? Why don't we just go down to breakfast?" Gideon suggested. Harriet could hear his stomach rumbling from where she stood. As was hers. But the idea had merit. They weren't prisoners in the castle and they could move around as they saw fit. Harriet reminded herself that she could take control of this situation, rather than just let things happen to her. When she had chosen that path in Verona, they had achieved the right outcome. She couldn't just let the tides of fate wash her around, eventually spitting her out at their whim.

Gideon was ready, his boots added to the new clothes from yesterday. They had both slept fully clothed, and Harriet didn't see the need to put the pearls back into her hair. She had pulled them out in the early hours of the morning, as the pins anchoring them in her hair had been digging viciously into her scalp.

"Breakfast it is," Harriet said, smiling a little at Gideon. Swinging the door open, Harriet sailed through it.

Straight into chaos. Their usually quiet corridor was full of castle servants hurrying back and forth. Although they were largely silent, there were so many of them that Harriet was surprised she hadn't known they were there. It was their faces that sent a shiver down Harriet's spine as they made their way slowly towards the stairs to the lower level. Each one revealed a look of frozen horror, their lips squeezed tightly shut and their complexions white. Harriet glanced at Gideon – from his set expression, he had noticed it too.

It wasn't long before they knew the reason for the change in the household staff. Walking into the great dining hall, the magnificently carved chairs at the head table caught their attention. But not for the usual reasons, such as the sparkle of the roughly cut emerald fixed into the apex of the King's chair, or the glow of rubies emanating from the Queen's seat. Rather, it was the black shrouds hung over the imposing symbols of power that captivated the eerily silent diners. There were plenty of them breaking their fasts, including many of the rough and ready fighting men they had seen over the last couple of days. But no-one spoke, no-one made eye contact.

Harriet looked at Gideon, horrified. Even being who they were, from another time and another place, the significance of the black material was not lost on them. The King was dead.

Gideon led them to the seats they had occupied the night before, at the end of the head table. On the one hand, it felt obscene to be sitting amongst the silent lords and laymen who made up Duncan's court – but on the other, where else were they to sit? Neither knew enough of etiquette in this time to choose an appropriate seat, so they were reliant on the advice of others to get them through. It turned out that they needn't have worried, as Lachlan received them rather gratefully as they took their places. He didn't say much, but his eyes showed that the strain of the extended silence was grating on his nerves and their company was a welcome distraction.

"Morning to yer both," Lachlan murmured as they settled into their seats. They mumbled their greetings back, Harriet unsure of what she said. Her attention swayed back and forth between the accusation that he wasn't his father's son, and the spectre that was the death of a monarch under this very roof. Her gaze darted around the hall, taking in the black fabric hanging from the wooden rafters far above her head. Aside from Lachlan and an ancient man at the other end, the main table was deserted. Harriet sat back as Gideon slid a plate in front of her unobtrusively. She had no idea what was on it, but she started picking away at the edges all the same. The only thing she remembered about any type of Scottish cuisine was haggis, and she couldn't remember what went into that. Which was probably a blessing. Harriet thought furiously as she delicately chased her food around the plate. How best to bring up the miasma of grief that was swirling around them as they ate?

In the end, Gideon took the bull by the horns. As he pushed back a little from the rough table, he asked Lachlan the all-important question in a low, dark voice. Lachlan sighed and angled himself a little more to face them.

"Tis King Duncan," Lachlan said, gesturing to the hauntingly grand chair. "When my father went to wake him 'tis morn to deal with the unrest in the north, he found the King lying dead. His chamberlains slept outside his door, horribly drunk from the night before." Lachlan glanced down at his hands before he continued, and Harriet saw him swallow hard. "My father killed every last one o' them, for their failure to protect oor king."

Harriet's eyes widened, and she could see Gideon's nostrils flare as he tried to control his reaction to the news. He didn't look surprised though, and Harriet knew this was because the story Lachlan told tallied with the original story of Macbeth. Only, they knew it wasn't some stranger who had snuck in and killed the King. It had been his own man, Macbeth. The person Lachlan thought was his father. Gideon might not be surprised, but Harriet was. She had snuck inside after the incident in the courtyard and it couldn't have been before one in the morning. Macbeth would have had to work fast to commit murder that night, and he hadn't seemed sure that he would do it when he slipped back through the door to the castle with his wife.

Harriet frowned. Yes, his wife. Gruoch had been quite vocal in her belief that Macbeth had to kill his king. And the mutterings she had heard while he'd been outside the stone walls…who did she want revenge on? Gruoch's words floated back to her, as if she were dreaming. Sisters, I challenge thee to stop me. Harriet frowned. Lady Macbeth had no sisters in the original play. Gideon had said so. Or at least, none that they knew of. They still hadn't solved the mystery of Lachlan's parentage.

You will not defeat me…His actions will avenge those wrongs done to me centuries ago. I will not rest until Duncan and all of kin pay for their treachery. What on earth had

Gruoch been talking about. And what was that purple light?

"Lachlan," Harriet said suddenly, disturbing the thoughts that the young man had lapsed into. He glanced up. "Does your mother have any sisters?" It was an oddly specific question, and Harriet scrambled to cover up her interest. "She's just been so lovely and welcoming. I wondered if all the ladies in Scotland were the same, or if your mother was one of a kind." It worked – Lachlan's attention had been deflected from the main question.

"No sisters," he murmured, taking a long draught from his cup of ale. "She is one of a kind. You know, my mother is one of those people who always thinks of others. When I was a little boy, she used to say to me 'a victory is nothing without honour, Lulach.'" Lachlan smiled fondly. The Gaelic version of his name tripped off his tongue in a lilting brogue that was hard to catch, but Harriet just made it out. Lachlan settled to tell stories of his mother, memories of his younger years at Inverness Castle with his parents. Including Lord Macbeth. Gideon listened intently, but Harriet couldn't stop her mind from wandering.

No sisters. So who on earth had she been speaking of the night before? It had seemed as though she had summoned the three women outside the stone walls…three women who sounded eerily familiar…. The realisation hit Harriet like a thunderbolt. She had met the three women before. In the forest, just before they had been taken hostage by Lachlan and his men. The lilting, almost musical voices. The silvery white light and the tinkling laughs. The women who had appeared outside the castle last night were the same women who had helped Harriet and Gideon on their arrival in this time. Harriet was as certain of it as she was that she would take another breath. Had Gruoch been referring to the fact that they were sisters, perhaps? Not that she had sisters herself.

More importantly, what had Duncan done to anger the Lady Macbeth? What could she possibly want revenge for? That was a question she couldn't ask Lachlan – not right on the heels of her last one, and especially not the morning after the King had shown up dead. Lachlan would essentially be giving his mother a motive for murdering their king, and Harriet doubted he would share anything with them of importance.

A commotion at one of the entrances to the great hall roused Harriet from her thoughts. She looked over to see Lord Macbeth striding towards their table, his face ashen and drawn.

He was halted halfway down the flagged length of the room by a middle aged man who had skidded to a halt in front of him. Harriet recognised him as a nobleman, from his place at the head table the night before.

"My Lord," he said, bowing low. Macbeth stared at him, a strange expression on his face. Lachlan sat up ramrod straight in his chair, his attention riveted to the spectacle playing out before them. Everyone in the hall was watching with bated breath.

"My Lord Macbeth," the man began again, his head raised a little from his position of obsequious prostration. "The Council of Lords has reached a decision about who should be King o' Scotland." The man crossed himself, his eyes flitting unbidden to the shrouding over the King's chair. He refocused. "The Lords have determined that it is ye, Lord Macbeth, Thane of Glamis and of Cawdor, who shall be King o' Scotland now. Long live King Macbeth." The man dropped his head again, waiting for a blessing from his new King.

The hall was completely still – in the stunned silence, the smallest shuffle of shoe on stone, the slightest scrape of hand on table was grotesquely audible. Everyone seemed to hold their collective breath as they waited for

Macbeth to reply – to respond in any way. So far, he hadn't moved a muscle. Except for the pulsating nerve in his jaw, everything about Macbeth was locked tight. His face was set in stone, more grey than white now, and he stood proud and tall but with haunted eyes. Those eyes finally flickered out, over the assembled company, judging and weighing the reaction to the news that had been brought from the Council.

"Arise, Lord Menteth," Macbeth almost pleaded, his voice low and gravelly. His head swivelled around as footsteps – heavy, ringing ones – sounded in the hallway beyond. Macbeth looked almost frightened, but then visibly relaxed as the other lords of the Council entered the hall.

"Yer Grace," they said, almost as one, sinking down onto their knees before a stunned Macbeth.

"But…what is the meaning of this?" stuttered Macbeth. He would almost be believable, if Harriet didn't know that he was responsible for the carnage around them. She tried hard to control the urge to roll her eyes.

"Yer Grace," the young man who had carried Harriet behind him on his horse as they travelled to Dunsinane stepped forward. He swept a low bow before continuing. "The

Council has decided that, in the absence of the late King's sons, Malcolm and Donalbain, ye are the best man to rule Scotland."

"For what reasons, Lord Angus?" Macbeth asked, his hands clasped in front of him. To Harriet it seemed as though he wanted confirmation of what he already knew. Perhaps he wanted his legitimacy for the throne declared before all of the court, so nobody could question his right to rule. It was a move that smacked of Gruoch, and Harriet quickly glanced around the hall. The lady was nowhere in sight. And Lord Angus? Harriet shook her head ruefully. She hadn't been sure that the young man who had ferried her to relative safety had been a nobleman, let alone a lord of the Council.

"Ye are cousin to King Duncan, God rest his soul," Lord Angus continued. "Ye also have a claim ter the throne through yer wife," he continued nervously. "Gruoch of Scotland – Lady Macbeth – is the granddaughter of King Kenneth III, God rest his soul." The hall seemed to cross itself as one. Lord Angus coughed nervously, and his eyes flitted to find those of his friend, seated next to Harriet at the main table. He steeled himself and continued.

"Begging yer pardon, yer Grace. Lady Gruoch was the only descendent of that royal family to survive the laws of transity – or rather, the attempt to avoid it. As her husband, and Duncan's cousin, ye have the strongest claim ter the throne. After ye, it would be Lulach." Angus' eyes sought out Lachlan once more. "But as yer know, Lulach's claim comes only through his mother's side and tisn't as strong." Angus coloured and pressed his lips tight together. Harriet eyed him as her brain tried desperately to absorb all of the information pooling around them, flowing through the main hall. There was so much here that they didn't know – or Harriet didn't know anyway – and how it would impact on the story they knew was anyone's guess. But they now knew for sure that Lachlan wasn't Macbeth's son, and that the people of Scotland knew it.

"Yer must prepare ter ride for Scone, yer Grace." Lord Angus was insistent.

"Ter be crowned," Macbeth murmured, his eyes seeking out his son in the rabble.

"Aye," Lord Angus replied.

Another lord with sandy blonde hair stepped up to stand beside Angus. "With yer Grace's permission," the lord bobbed his head. "I wish to return to Fife as soon as I can. With the unrest in the north, I'm sure ye will understand my haste?" Macbeth regarded him steadily, but the toughened lord held his own.

"Very well, Lord Macduff," the new King said slowly. "Ye shall return ter Fife to settle the unrest. The rest of us shall ride fer Scone Abbey an hour from now."

"What about the coronation banquet?" Lachlan enquired, finally rising from his seat and lending his voice to the conversation.

"Aye," Macbeth replied, his brow furrowed. "Ye mother will wish ter be present for that. I'm sure she would wish it to be held at Inverness, at oor home. But tis best it be held here, as we have the late king ter lay ter rest, after all. With the unrest in the north, we cannae have Scotland without a crowned king." Macbeth swivelled to face the crowd of faces that had been avidly watching the exchange. "Bring me Fraser," his voice commanded, bouncing off the dark, smooth walls of the hall and echoing around the rafters. "He will take charge of Duncan's body." Macbeth turned on his heel, intending to quit the hall. At the last moment, he locked eyes with Lachlan and beckoned with his head for him to follow. Lachlan excused himself with a murmur, following in his father's wake as he disappeared into the shadowy hallways that snaked all around the great hall.

Harriet sat back in her seat, wide-eyed. Her brain whirred as it stored memories and information, neatly filed to retrieve later on as she needed. Harriet had always had one of those brains – one that could retain almost all of the information that made its way inside. Her memory was superb, and she was a sharp and intelligent young woman. Strangely, just having Gideon beside her felt comforting. He didn't touch her at all, but she could feel his presence wrapping around her like a warm blanket.

"We need to get out of here," Gideon murmured in her ear, his breath washing over her neck. Harriet suppressed a shiver. Nodding, Harriet pushed her chair back, its feet protesting with a screech as it slid over the cobbled floor.

"We need to get in on that coronation," Harriet whispered to Gideon as they hurried from the hall.

"Do you think we'll learn something valuable there?" Gideon mumbled back as they hurried up the stairs to their room.

"Perhaps," Harriet replied. "But I've also never seen a royal coronation." She smiled a little sadly. "And as the king is already dead, I suppose there's no one to save here."

Chapter Fourteen

"You can't save everyone, Harry," Gideon murmured to Harriet, seated in front of him on a stocky Scottish pony. He had his arm around her waist to anchor her to the saddle, and she squeezed his forearm with her hand to show she had heard his words.

Despite the comfort she heard in his tone, she didn't feel any better about the outcome of the story so far. She felt as though she was meant to go back in time to help people – to save them. The sisters in the woods had said there was death coming to their land. Trouble, strife, upheaval. Surely there was no greater example of that than the death of their king. And Harriet had failed to stop it.

So sunk into her thoughts was she that she hadn't noticed Gideon's use of her nickname for the first time. As they plodded through the countryside, Harriet couldn't fail to notice the scenery, despite her preoccupation. It was, quite simply, gorgeous. The swaying fields of purple heather seemed endless – jewel-like and winking in the late morning sun. The sky was impossibly blue, but she should see storm clouds on the horizon that seemed to echo her mood. The air here seemed thicker than home, the blue dome above their heads closer and easier to reach. The soaring skies of Australia seemed like a lifetime ago, despite the relatively short time they'd spent in Scotland so far. With a sharp pang, Harriet thought about her family. She hadn't missed them as quickly this time around, perhaps because she had Gideon to distract her. Dealing with his reaction to moving through a time rift had consumed her time and her thoughts.

Harriet didn't want him to think she was weird, especially after they had returned to their own time. She had to believe that they would. As she had last time, Harriet missed her mother's smile, her father's laughter. She even missed her brothers' bickering, though perhaps not as keenly as the first two. Mason would love this adventure – Harriet could almost see his sparkling eyes and cheeky smile. He would have been in the thick of it, looking at everything and everyone. He would especially love that Gideon was here...Gideon always had time for Mason, even if they hadn't seen each other much the last few years. Mason was football mad, and Gideon was like a god or hero to him. He worshipped the ground he walked on.

Tristan would not be quite as enthused, Harriet mused, her attention scattering like pollen on the winds that blew gently across the hills and hollows. The older of her two brothers had matured quite a lot recently, even though Mason pulled him back to his mischievous self every now and again. Harriet knew he'd be more cautious than his little brother, more wary of the people who surrounded them and the situation they were in. Imagine if it had been Tristan who had come back with her, rather than Gideon.

That would have been a little harder to explain, Harriet thought ruefully. Although we wouldn't be having to dodge a fake marriage ceremony. Harriet sighed. On the bright side, that whole sideshow was likely to be sidelined in the wake of the death of Duncan.

"What are you thinking?" Gideon murmured in her ear.

"Nothing," Harriet replied, a little too quickly. She felt rather than heard his chuckle. Harriet was beginning to suspect that Gideon knew how much he affected her, and she felt even more self-conscious about it. Their extremely close proximity on the back of this horse wasn't helping at all.

It had been surprisingly easy to convince Lord and Lady Macbeth – the soon to be crowned King and Queen – to take them along for the coronation. Harriet had expressed an interest in wanting to see the difference between Scottish and English royal tradition and Macbeth's Scottish pride had done the rest. He had his other man, Fletcher, saddle the stocky little pony that was left in the stables. With most of the court riding alongside them, there hadn't been any other horses to spare.

The sight of the lords and ladies of Scotland pouring over the ranges of heather and mist in their finery was breathtaking. Everyone was in black – as was proper to mourn the man found dead in his bed just that morning – but the Scottish did mourning well. Gruoch's voluminous black silk skirts shone darkly in the summer sunshine. Her hair was bundled up under a veil, and the train of her skirt appeared to be longer than usual – perhaps that was a queenly custom? They were riding for Lia Fail or "the speaking stone", as some of the household staff had whispered about before they had left. Gideon said it was also called the Stone of Destiny, because it had been used to unite the Scots and Pictish kingdoms. It also apparently decided who the next king was to be, atop Moot Hill near the

Scone Abbey. Centuries of Scottish kings had been crowned in the same place and it was the ancient tradition of the land they were in.

Truth be told, Harriet was a little excited to see it. Her experience of coronations was non-existent, having never seen one in her own lifetime. She'd seen some televised royal weddings, and the pomp and pageantry had been impressive. Like most little girls, she'd once dreamed of growing up and marrying her Prince Charming. That dream was still there, but it was buried a little under the hopes and dreams Harriet had for herself and her own future. She wanted to be somebody, to be important and needed. Not just a wife and mother. Sure, one day those things too. Just not yet.

Shaking herself, Harriet recalled her attention to the present. They had been travelling for nearly two hours, and the sun was high in the sky. They couldn't be far from Scone – Lachlan had said it wasn't an arduous ride, and they would be back in time for the coronation feast that night. Harriet stroked a hand over the smooth material of the black gown Lady Macbeth had loaned to her for the mourning period, and she supposed, the coronation. It was of much finer material than the gown given to her by the sisters in the woods. The gown wasn't as rich in colour as the other that King Duncan had gifted to her, but if black was required, black she would wear. This dress was also made of wool as fine and soft as the beautiful green gown that had once belonged to Duncan's queen. The sleeves were flared and cut artistically to hang down her wrists to the point of the snug undersleeves that hugged her arms. Although the dress was a little long for Harriet, she was much the same build as Lady Macbeth and the fabric hugged her curves, as it was designed to do. The skirts flared out, full and flowing. Gideon's face had closed off when he'd caught sight of her in the castle courtyard, just before she'd been handed up to their horse. He had already been seated astride, ready to steady her as she gained purchase on the pony's back. Gideon was dressed head to toe in black as well.

"Where did your clothes come from," Harriet murmured as the thought occurred to her.

"Lachlan," Gideon whispered back. "Little tight around the shoulders, but a good fit otherwise." Harriet couldn't disagree. On the horizon, Harriet could see a hill rising from the ground surrounding it. It couldn't be long now.

And it wasn't. Within the hour, Harriet was sliding down from the back of the pony, helped by Gideon who had dismounted first. Harriet liked this little pony – it was solid and dependable, and didn't seem likely to bolt on them. Harriet stroked her nose as she walked past, smiling affectionately. She was definitely getting better with horses.

The lords of the court were milling around, tying their mounts to the trees dotted around the hill – what must be Moot Hill. Atop it, Harriet could see what looked like a simple block of stone – the Stone of Destiny? Harriet frowned. It was rather plain for something so portentous.

Macbeth emerged from the small Abbey set alongside the base of the hill, three monks and an obviously more senior cleric in tow. As Harriet watched, Macbeth went to his horse and produced something from the bag strapped to the animal's back. It glittered as the sunlight struck it.

Macbeth made his way back to the men in plain robes, standing with their hands one atop the other. Harriet looked more closely and saw there were two simple, golden diadems in his hands, one slighter larger than the other. They were to crown two monarchs today. Harriet tried not to think about how Macbeth had come by the crowns.

Without speaking, the monks gestured for the assembled crowd to ascend the small hill to the stone perched on top. Leading the procession were the future King and Queen themselves, followed by Lachlan and Lord Angus.

Taking their seats upon the blackened stone, Lord and Lady Macbeth stared back at the most powerful lords and ladies of their land. It was unreal to watch – like a play or movie unfolding before their eyes. Then the sounds of the coronation began, as the monks started chanting and speaking, their voices musical and lilting. Harriet strained to hear, but she couldn't understand their words. It sounded like another language, albeit a beautiful one.

"They're speaking in Gaelic," Gideon murmured, his voice almost soundless. He was patently in awe, and when Harriet stopped to think about it, she realised how amazing it was to be standing in this moment. They were in Macbeth, at the apex of the tragedy, right before everything else went very wrong for the upstart family. This was the happiest they would be for the rest of their lives, according to Shakespeare's play. A part of Harriet's heart felt heavy for the doomed couple, but then she remembered the events of the night before and her face hardened. She hadn't been able to prevent them from killing Duncan. What then, was her purpose here? It wasn't to feel sorry for sociopathic killers.

The ceremony was quick and meaningful, the reverence palpable on the hill. Their traditions and customs may have been simple, but they held deep significance for the people of this country. Lord and Lady Macbeth – their Graces – swept back down Moot Hill as crowned sovereigns. Exchanging pleasantries, and Harriet would swear some gold coins, the new monarchs led the company in taking their leave of the Abbey's monks. Everyone remounted their horses for the trip back to Dunsinane.

"That was quick." Harriet's voice floated back to Gideon, behind her again on their pony. He agreed quietly.

"Harriet," Gideon said urgently, his voice low but clear. "Duncan was meant to be killed at Inverness, according to the story. But he was murdered at Dunsinane."

"So?" Harriet frowned. "Easy enough for a location to change in an ancient story."

"It's not following the pattern that it should," Gideon insisted. "That means the rest of the story might not follow the pattern."

Harriet frowned. "What are you trying to say?"

"Macbeth's best friend, Banquo…" Gideon pointed discreetly to the man riding to the left of the new king. "He is the next to die…and his murder is arranged in the afternoon or twilight hours before the coronation banquet starts. His son, Fleance, escapes and flees Scotland."

Harriet's heart lurched. Two deaths in 24 hours would certainly be a failure on her part. Aside from the needless loss of life, what would such a failure mean for their ability to return home? Much as she was enjoying the gowns, the scenery and Gideon's company, 11th century Scotland was not a place she wanted to dwell in for much longer.

"What do we do?" Harriet hissed, thinking more aloud than speaking to anyone else.

"We need to warn Banquo," Gideon said, his voice confident. Harriet thought about that. A warning from two strangers – foreigners from another country no less – about one's best friend intending to kill them. Who would she believe? Well…not her own best friend just now. But Banquo was unlikely to take their warning seriously.

"No," Harriet said slowly. "We need to talk to Macbeth himself. I need to talk to Macbeth."

"Absolutely not," Gideon growled. "That's insanely dangerous."

Harriet bristled. Gideon's tone suggested that his hesitance was due to her being a woman, rather than anything about her ability. She wondered if he might be so against it if she had suggested he speak with Macbeth. Likely not. Harriet opened her mouth to retort, when Gideon continued.

"The man has just killed his own king. What do you think he would do to us?" Harriet's ire calmed at his use of the word 'us'. It wasn't just her, then. Despite his worry, which wasn't unjustified, Harriet knew in her gut that this was what she had to do. She knew that Macbeth was being controlled by his wife…to what extent she wasn't sure. Harriet knew with instinctive certainty that the key to stopping the chain of events that was about to happen was to break Gruoch's hold over her husband. As they plodded back to Dunsinane, Harriet plotted and planned her approach and what she would say. She discarded strategy after strategy, until she finally settled on one that she thought had some chance of success.

"Gideon," Harriet murmured as they climbed the last of the hill to the castle proper. "You need to go and keep an eye on Banquo."

"Split up?" Gideon said, his tone conveying his anxiety at the idea.

"Yes," Harriet said firmly. "It's necessary, and I'll be fine. You'll be fine."

As she slid down from the horse in the keep, Harriet caught and held Gideon's gaze.

"We will do this. Together."

Chapter Fifteen

Macbeth made it easier than Harriet could have dreamed to gain an audience with him that afternoon. The lords and ladies had been instructed to do whatever took their fancy until the daylight faded. When they reached deep twilight, the banquet would begin and the court would come back together. They had about two hours left before that happened.

Harriet crept her way through the dark halls of Dunsinane castle, searching for signs of where she might find Macbeth himself. She peeked into room after room, an excuse ready on her tongue for anyone she might meet inside. They were all empty though and she had no need of her invented reasons.

Finally, Harriet made her way to the end of the lower hallway, almost directly beneath their own room. Lady Macbeth's sitting room was halfway down this corridor and Harriet had already passed it. She could see light flickering from underneath the heavy wooden floor shielding the last room in the corridor. Harriet was grateful that Lady Macbeth had not been in the rooms she had already checked – Gruoch was the very last person Harriet wanted to see just now.

Setting her hand to the ringed handle, Harriet pushed against the ancient wooden door and it creaked open. Peering around the edge of the door, Harriet looked into the room. It was as richly furnished as all the others. A large desk stood in pride of place in the centre of the room and a fire flickered in the hearth. Warmth permeated the room, making it inviting after the dank, icy hallways. Most importantly though was the man seated at the desk, gazing into the fire as if he wasn't seeing anything in front of him. Just who she was looking for.

Harriet cleared her throat and Lord Macbeth – King Macbeth – looked up, startled. His face relaxed as he saw Harriet, and a small smile softened the harsh lines of his face.

"Ach, Lady Harriet," Macbeth said, gesturing for her to enter the room. Harriet did so, closing the door behind her.

"Please, sit," he invited. Harriet took one of the well stuffed chairs in front of his imposing desk. Macbeth sat back in his seat, pressing his fingers together under his chin in a prayer position. He tapped his jaw as he studied Harriet through hooded eyes.

"What can I do for yer, my Lady?" Macbeth asked.

Harriet had thought long and hard about what she should say, and how. How should she approach a man who had just killed another, who had spoken to spirits the night before and was now a crowned king? Harriet thought she would talk about the one thing that hadn't changed – his marriage. And given she was expected to soon enter her own, as far as they knew, asking about it would seem a natural thing to do.

"I wished to speak with you about marriage," Harriet stated, watching as panic raced over Macbeth's face. It would be amusing, if it weren't such a serious situation they were in.

"Ah," he stalled. "Tis that a question better suited ter my wife?" Panic, loud and clear. Harriet smirked inside.

"Well you see, your Grace," Harriet said, innocence infused through her tone. "Lady Macbeth – her Grace – has seemed so tired lately. Surely you've noticed it. Why, in just the short time I've been here, I've noticed her becoming more and more weary. I didn't think it proper to bother her just now." Harriet watched Macbeth through her lashes, her eyes downcast. He was frowning. Then he cleared his throat.

"Ach well. I thought perhaps I was just imaginin' things," he said, his voice low. "But if ye have noticed it too…maybe tis not the case." He sighed heavily. "Gruoch has not seemed…herself, since we left Inverness. Tis almost like she's another person some days. Then others she is so tired, tis almost as though she cannae sleep." Macbeth's brow furrowed. Harriet's did as well. She hadn't expected that. She had been trying to lead Macbeth into questioning his wife's influence, but it seemed as though he already had concerns about her in another sense.

"This business about the crowning has opened old wounds," the King said heavily, his face downcast.

"What wounds?" Harriet almost whispered. She was afraid to say more, in case Macbeth stopped talking.

"I am nae Gruoch's first husband," Macbeth said. 'Tis common enough knowledge round these parts. Lulach – Lachlan – tis not my son. This decision about who inherits has pulled Gruoch in two directions. She is of the old ruling house – the last descendent. The rest were murdered or killed." Harriet squirmed uncomfortably, unsure of how to react.

"That makes Lulach the last o' his line, but through his mother," Macbeth continued. "Which is what made my claim stronger. But fer Gruoch, seeing Duncan as King was hard. His family stole hers. And she is my wife, but seeing me as King, well…," Macbeth trailed off, his concerned unvoiced, but nevertheless hanging in the air between them, laden with meaning. Lots of little bits and pieces that had been missing from the fabric of the story wove into place with Macbeth's words. That could explain Gruoch's animosity towards Duncan, and her desire to see him pay. Her performance in the courtyard had just seemed a little too vicious for a third generation descendent.

Harriet jumped violently as the door flung open behind her, rocking back on its hinges and hitting the grey wall beside it. Framed in the doorway was Lady Macbeth, and her face was a harbinger of the storm that was about to break on Harriet's head. She had the unnerving feeling that Gruoch knew she had been asking questions she shouldn't, or receiving information she wasn't entitled to. Even Lord Macbeth looked nervous.

"What is the meaning of this?" Gruoch's tone was commanding, her eyes shooting daggers at Harriet. Moving fluidly, she crossed the room to stand at the side of her husband's desk, effectively between Harriet and her husband.

"Lady Harriet was just discussing…marriage," Macbeth finished lamely, falling back on Harriet's excuse.

"With ye?" Gruoch asked incredulously, an eyebrow raised.

"I suppose," Macbeth mumbled. He was avoiding his wife's eyes, and Harriet couldn't blame him. She was trying to as well.

"Lady Harriet and I will talk in my rooms," Lady Macbeth said imperiously. Her eyes were fixed on Harriet, and she felt compelled to move with Gruoch, despite her desire not to. It almost seemed as though Harriet wasn't in control of her own limbs. They felt heavy and didn't seem to be obeying her brain, which was screaming at her to run.

Like a lamb to the slaughter, Harriet followed Lady Macbeth out of the room. Gruoch swept down the corridor like a ship at full sail. Her steps were precise and crisp, her shoes echoing on the stone floors. Despite the sense of impending doom, Harriet couldn't think of a way to escape. They passed Lady Macbeth's sitting room and took another turn, one that Harriet remembered well. Her mind started to scream, telling her to move, get away, run –

anything! But her legs marched on, despite her will to retreat.

Gruoch started down the spiral staircase that Harriet knew led to the cellars. Without having to lift a finger to compel her, Lady Macbeth towed Harriet in her wake. How was she doing that? Panic started to claw at Harriet as the gaping door to the darkness of the cellar prison stood before her.

When Lady Macbeth turned to face her, Harriet's blood ran cold.

"Get inside," Gruoch said, her voice cold. Her eyes were like flint, black and unwelcoming. Her pale, beautiful face was expressionless, but her gaze conveyed how furious she was. Again, Harriet tried to move against the compulsion to enter the room, but she couldn't control her own limbs.

"I thought ye might be useful," Gruoch said coldly. "Something ter play with, ter torment my sisters with. They thought ye could stop Macbeth, save Duncan, Banquo and all of the others who must die ter ensure that I have my revenge." She sneered. "And I so would have looked forward ter a wedding." Gruoch's tone left Harriet in no doubt she and Gideon were exposed as frauds. Gruoch had known all along that they weren't who they said they were.

"Now ye will stay here until my plan is carried out, and my retribution is completed." Gruoch turned away to grasp the edge of the door, intending to slam it on Harriet.

"He will look for me," Harriet said, her voice quavering despite her insistence that it remain strong.

"The boy ye came with?" Gruoch laughed, low and cold. "He will nae live much longer. He's in my way now. Any other questions?"

Harriet thought furiously. She needed to keep Gruoch talking. If she was going to die in this cellar, she'd at least go down fighting. Harriet couldn't seem to control her limbs, but she could still think and speak.

"Actually, yes," Harriet said. She saw Gruoch pause. "What was the purple light?"

"None of ye business," Lady Macbeth sneered. The question had snuck under her guard though. She clearly didn't know Harriet had possessed that knowledge.

"What do you know of three sisters? They're very beautiful, kind-hearted. Extraordinarily silvery and shimmery." Harriet took a stab in the dark, and it paid off. Gruoch froze, and her face turned thunderous.

"Those are my sisters," Gruoch retorted hotly. "They are weak," she spat at Harriet. "They could take revenge with me, destroy the ruling family who tore oor country apart, but they are feeble." Gruoch's black eyes flashed – they were scary and unworldly in her uncontrolled fury.

"But," Harriet said, her voice as innocent as she could make it. "You have no sisters, Lady Macbeth?"

Gruoch jeered, and her face turned ugly and twisted. "I am nae Lady Macbeth. Her body, her appearance, was useful ter get what I wanted. Which was ter get close ter Macbeth, and ter twist the prophecy my sisters gave him. Lady Macbeth will be destroyed before I am done. Such a kind heart…tis a pity to crush it." Gruoch – or whoever it was inside her – laughed, the sound chilling.

"So if you're not Lady Macbeth…or Gruoch…what are you called?" Harriet asked, sounding much braver than she felt. She could feel the anger swirling in the air, red and pulsing from the being inside Lady Macbeth.

"Cailleach," she said shortly. "Not that ye'll live long enough to have any use of it." With that, Cailleach slammed the door to the cellar shut, and Harriet heard the bolt slide closed before the footsteps faded away, leaving her in the dark and silence.

Harriet sat down heavily on a barrel. She seemed to have control of her limbs once more, though they were as shaky as an autumn leaf dangling from the bare branches of a wintering tree.

"Didn't see that coming," Harriet murmured to herself. Resting her chin on her upturned palm, Harriet tried to focus and absorb everything. It was the only thing keeping her from panicking in the dark.

She was trapped. And if Cailleach had her way, Gideon wouldn't be coming for her. Harriet knew without a doubt that Cailleach would do anything she could to stop Macbeth being diverted from his current course. Banquo was going to die: Macbeth, ultimately, would die. As would Lady Macbeth. But it hadn't been their own greed and ambition that had caused their untimely demises. Rather, it was the whim of one very angry spirit. A tragedy indeed.

How could someone so dark be sister to three so full of light? Harriet mused to herself as she tried to ignore the shadows that were deepening as night fell.

Shaking herself out of her thoughts, Harriet tried to concentrate on what she could do to get out of her prison. She felt sure that Cailleach was confident Harriet was contained. Otherwise, her limbs would not be hers to control. Harriet needed to reach

Gideon before Cailleach did – that now took priority over anything else, including saving more innocent lives from being crushed by Cailleach's machinations. Without Gideon, she didn't know if she could return home. She couldn't – wouldn't – return without him in any event.

Harriet looked around for a way out. She remembered Gideon tracing around the cellar in the gloaming when they had arrived, looking for a weakness: a door, window – anything that would connect them with the outside world. The heavy main door was useless: Harriet had heard the bolt scrape home. She tried it anyway, in case, but wasn't surprised when it didn't budge an inch. Rather than waste her effort on useless panic or frustration, Harriet began to methodically work her way around the walls of the cellar, pressing stones and the cracks between them, wedging her fingers into tiny crevices and corners. Blowing out a breath, Harriet realised she was back where she had started. There was no secret exit, like in the adventure movies she'd watched with her father. There was no hero to come sweeping in to save her, like in the romance novels Tessa favoured. She was on her own.

Harriet tried to think of what her mother would do if she were in the same situation. Harriet smiled a little. Her mother would probably write a list of pros and cons for every possible reaction to this scenario, then choose the best fit. With no pen or paper, Harriet would have to improvise.

There were no windows, yet she had fresh air. Sure, it was a little stale this far down in the castle, but it was more musty than suffocating. There had to be air coming from somewhere other than just the cracks around the main door. In the gathering gloom, Harriet could still just discern the outlines of the barrels stacked against the far wall. The floor seemed to slope upwards them, which struck Harriet as a little odd. Tilting her head to the side, Harriet bit down on her bottom lip. Could she move the barrels to check? Would she be wasting her energy and oxygen?

Harriet shook her head disbelievingly. Maybe she was light on air. She was going to die down here if she didn't do something soon. And Gideon would die up there. Squaring her shoulders, Harriet began to wrestle the nearest barrel out of its neat line. It hadn't been so bad: she had rolled it on its bottom the way she'd seen her father do at home. Smiling grimly, Harriet rolled barrel after barrel out of the way until she could see behind them. Her smile widened as she saw a rectangular glimmer of light. Maybe the adventure films weren't all that far-fetched, after all. It was an air vent of sorts, but it was very small. Given that it was surrounded by stone, Harriet knew there would be no give in it. She would either fit, or she wouldn't.

Assessing the space, measuring it in her head, Harriet knew that it would be a tight squeeze. Glancing down at the dress she wore – which now felt itchy and poisonous given who it had come from – she tried to determine the best way to make herself smaller. The material was slippery, so it might give her an advantage in crawling or sliding through the space, but the skirts were too big. Biting her lip, Harriet gathered the skirts in her hands and ripped. The sound of rending fabric ripped through the still air as Harriet defaced the beautiful mourning dress. She stopped when it sat just above her knees, rather than half a metre past her toes. Taking a deep breath, Harriet crouched down and reached one arm through the hole. She could feel the night air on her arm, the breeze against her skin as she worked to fit the rest of her body through the narrow gap.

Harriet was doing well, until she got to her hips. She had known they would be the hardest part, and she had her arms well clear now. They would help to get leverage against the stone wall. Praying as hard as she could that the slippery material would help, Harriet put all her might into pushing herself away from her rock prison. In a shush of material, Harriet went tumbling into the courtyard. Quickly gathering herself, she shrank back into the shadows against the castle walls.

She had to find Gideon before Cailleach did.

Chapter Sixteen

The lights from the main hall spilled out through the open doors, the open windows, into the courtyard of the castle. The sounds of laughter, music, dancing and revelry reached through into the night, celebrating the coronation of a man who had murdered his predecessor.

Unwittingly, Harriet thought to herself as she crouched in the shadows. But he still did it. She could feel the impending sense of doom pressing down on her – the fracturing of time that seemed to stand still and rush past at the same moment. Harriet knew she wouldn't have all that long before Cailleach realised she had escaped. If she went to check on her captive at any point, Harriet didn't think it would take much for Cailleach to locate her. She was other worldly, and it was clear that she was powerful. In an evil way, but that just made her more intimidating.

Harriet looked up sharply at the sound of heavy footsteps outside the castle walls. They sounded unsteady, as though the person in charge of them was inebriated, and Harriet curled herself into a tiny ball as the hidden door in the wall sprang open.

In the darkness, it was hard for Harriet to see who was entering the castle. Clearly, it was someone who knew how to sneak out and in. As the moon sailed out from behind a dense cloud, the man's face was illuminated for a brief moment in blinding white reflection.

Banquo. Harriet recognised the face of the man that laid claim to Macbeth's dearest friendship. He had been attacked, and he was sporting a jagged cut across his forehead. Harriet noticed he was cradling his right arm, and a dark red stain spread out across his upper arm from a gash that had also ripped open his dark tunic sleeve. The uneven footsteps had been his.

Behind Banquo came another man that Harriet didn't recognise, but he was young and had the look of his father. He was also nursing injuries. It wasn't difficult to see that this was Fleance – the resemblance to Banquo was too great to ignore.

Harriet's heart leapt as she remembered her instructions to Gideon. Protect Banquo. Protect Fleance. Here they were, bloodied but alive. Perhaps then…Gideon might be with them. Gideon might still be alive.

Harriet's prayers were answered as a third man entered the castle keep. The silhouette was now as familiar to her as her own – the messy dark hair, broad shoulders and narrow waist. Harriet stifled a cry of relief as Gideon's face hove into view. It was quickly doused as she saw the injuries he'd sustained. His nose was bloodied, his right cheek bleeding onto his collar.

Harriet moved as swiftly as she could through the shadows of the courtyard. She had to get to the men before they went inside, or all would be lost. As soon as Cailleach saw Gideon, and perhaps even Banquo and Fleance, she would know her planning had been for nought. Harriet fetched up alongside Gideon – he was tired, and she managed to sneak through the dark to his side without him seeing her. She didn't want to startle an exclamation from him, so she put her hand over his mouth, willing him to be silent.

Gideon was injured, but not that badly. He spun around and grabbed her, holding her defensively so she couldn't move. Harriet remained still. The other two men had spun to see their companion's attacker as well.

"Jesus, Harriet," Gideon exhaled in relief. "Don't do that again." Harriet nodded, then touched his face gingerly where his wounds showed.

"What happened?"

"We were set upon on the moors," Banquo growled, clutching his arm. "The lad here thinks it were Macbeth who arranged the assassins. They're sleeping with the fishes now, thanks to yer man here." Gideon had coloured a little as Banquo had spoken, and the moonlight was sufficient for Harriet to see it.

"I'll nae believe it until I see his face fer meself," Banquo scowled, turning back towards the castle.

"Wait!" Harriet said, her voice low but her tone urgent. She crept out of the shadows into the moonlight, still wary of being seen. All three men stared at her, their eyes bulging out of their heads.

"Harry!" Gideon exclaimed. He swept off the cloak he was wearing. "What happened to your dress?" He swung the cloak over Harriet's shoulders, effectively screening her from view. Banquo and Fleance had looked away discreetly, embarrassment evident in their faces.

"Harry's a strange name for a girl," Banquo muttered under his breath.

"Mock me later," Harriet retorted, not without a little heat. "My dress is ruined because I've been locked in the cellar. The same cellar we were thrown in when we got here." Harriet turned to Gideon. His face was like a thundercloud.

"I told you we shouldn't have separated," he snarled. Harriet shushed him urgently. "It was Macbeth, wasn't it?" He demanded.

Harriet shook her head adamantly. "No, Gideon. We're wrong. It's not Macbeth who is behind all of this. It's his wife. Or rather, someone using his wife."

Gideon frowned. So did Banquo and Fleance. "What do you mean, 'using his wife'?" Gideon asked. "We know that Lady Macbeth convinces her husband to do things he shouldn't…." Harriet was shaking her head again. "No, it's more than that," she said, her tone insistent and urgent.

As quickly as she could, without omitting any details she could remember, Harriet relayed her visit to Lord Macbeth, her encounter with Lady Macbeth and her discovery of Cailleach. As she tried to say her name, the unfamiliar syllables tying her tongue and tripping her up, Banquo's eyes grew wide. He crossed himself and muttered something in Gaelic. Fleance rapidly followed.

"What?" Gideon demanded. "What does the name mean to you?"

Banquo looked like a frightened little boy, despite the hardened exterior of his military trained body.

"Cailleach 'tis an old name, one that is associated with the darkest of magicks," Banquo said, his voice shaking. "Even saying her name can be dangerous." His eyes were wide in the dark, the whites of them gleaming against the blackened backdrop of night.

"Well stop saying it," Harriet hissed, in no desire to meet the lady – spirit – herself again any time soon. "What do we do?"

Fleance frowned. "You say that C – she is in Lady Macbeth's body?"

"Yes!" Harriet replied, exasperated. "And that tallies with Lord Macbeth's remarks just before she came storming in that Gruoch hasn't been herself since they left Inverness."

Banquo's eyes widened, and he groaned as if he were in pain. Alarmed, Harriet sprang forward to help him, her eyes fixed on the wound on his arm. Perhaps the cut was deeper than it looked…

"'Tis not that," Banquo said, waving her away. "I was with Macbeth and Gruoch when they travelled from Inverness. I heard the first prophecy, at Sueno's Stone, just south of Inverness. Gruoch had lagged behind, and Macbeth and I were at the crossroads waiting fer her ter catch up. The three sisters – beautiful they were – appeared at the stone and told their prophecy. Macbeth was ter be king, and my sons were ter father generations of kings ter come. It didn't make much sense at the time and we laughed it off – Macbeth was unlikely ter inherit with Duncan having two sons, and…," Banquo trailed off, his mouth twisting in horror as his memories collided together to form a whole picture.

"No," he breathed. "He wouldnae."

"We think Macbeth killed King Duncan," Gideon said with a grimace. "But it seems he was more influenced by Gruoch than any of us could ever have known."

"Tis a legend around these parts," Banquo almost whispered. "The kings come from the Houses of Dunkeld and Alpin are cursed. Cailleach…there was a girl. She was alive at the time of Kenneth III. Legend says that her heart was broken when the man she loved spurned her fer another woman. That woman went on ter become the Queen of Scotland, and the lass died of a broken heart. She is said ter have haunted the royal bloodlines since. Of course, most people dismiss it as nonsense and fancy. But some say that is how the spirit of Cailleach was twisted and corrupted. She was originally of the Four – light spirits who protect people. O' course," Banquo continued with a shrug. "The kings of those houses often murdered each other, intent on having power for themselves. Who's to say what's right." Banquo's voice trailed off into the night as he lapsed into his thoughts.

Harriet glanced at Gideon. They had already stopped the story as it was meant to play out. Banquo was meant to be dead, and Fleance fleeing to safety in another country. They might have stopped the assassins from taking Banquo, but had they led them into even greater danger? If Fleance was to father a line of kings, and he died instead, would the future of the Scottish monarchy be wiped out?

Butterfly effects made Harriet's brain ache – which was ironic given her new role in moving between time rifts. Blowing out a breath, Harriet looked up into the night sky to clear her head and order her thoughts. Staring at the stars, her eyes fixated on the pulsing blue one that she had seen the other nights they had spent in Scotland.

"Gideon," she murmured, grabbing his hand. "The star is still there."

"I haven't seen it before," Gideon replied, squeezing her hand. "At least, not before we came through…," he realised where he was and who was listening. "Just before we reached Scotland was the first time I saw it. Near the river that we know so well."

Harriet picked up his code easily enough. He had seen it while they were near the Derwent, in Tasmania, the twilight evening they had crossed through this time. Harriet studied the glowing orb. It had moved again, and it was almost aligned with two others stars that pulsed with the same colour, only much fainter and smaller in size. They formed almost a perfect line, as they had the night of the Derwent Dip. Weird.

"So…what are ye going ter do?" Banquo asked, wincing as he shifted his injured arm.

What could they do? Although they'd saved these two, Lord and Lady Macbeth were still in peril. Gruoch in particular, if the stories of Cailleach that Banquo had told them were true.

"We have to fight," Harriet said simply. "Hopefully not until we actually need to, but if you want to save Macbeth from certain death, we will need to do something. I would suggest first, that we sneak into the stables and patch all three of you up. You are little use as you are just now, and we'll need all the strength we can get.

The ragged little band of survivors crept into the shadows of the stables, Banquo grumbling that he'd never had to sneak anywhere in his life. Fleance silenced his father with a curt remark and a look, and Banquo had the grace to look sheepish.

Harriet sat and reflected as the men took long drinks of water from skeins that had been boiled and prepared for their travels earlier that day. She had no desire to face Cailleach again any time soon. Harriet was under no illusions that the next time they met, Cailleach would be taking no prisoners. In the dark depths of Lady Macbeth's eyes earlier that evening, Harriet had seen the spark of madness, of restrained glee at the suffering of others. Cailleach wouldn't be giving up on her revenge without a fight, and they had no idea what she was capable of, or what she really wanted from them.

Revenge on Duncan's line, Harriet thought. That tallied with what Banquo had said. You will not stop me, sisters. Harriet jerked upright on her hay bale.

The sisters had appeared to them when they had needed it most, and they had appeared to Macbeth when he had summoned them. Or

Cailleach had summoned them. Harriet frowned. Either way, they'd appeared. She hoped it wasn't the latter, because she didn't think Cailleach would be open to summoning assistance to destroy herself. Harriet's shoulders slumped again as she realised that she had absolutely no idea how to conjure a spirit. Until three hours ago, she hadn't truly believed in them. But no one who had faced the unveiled evil in Lady Macbeth's face when Cailleach shone herself through could mistake what they were looking at. Gideon had also seen the light that heralded the arrival and departure of the three sisters, so she hadn't imagined that. And she had heard their voices herself: light, tinkling and familiar.

In a flash of clarity, Harriet saw the book. The old, browning book with Shakespeare's notes in it. If that didn't have something in it about conjuring spirits, what were they even doing here? The man was the master of a good supernatural scene.

"Gideon," Harriet hissed, waving him over. He prowled across the floor towards her. "We need to sneak up into our room and get the book," she breathed, just loud enough for his ears only. Gideon regarded her steadily, then reached into his tunic. Out came the book.

"You mean this one?" he said with a grin.

Harriet smiled with delight, and took the ageing book gingerly from Gideon. Cradling it between her hands, she noticed that Gideon had shifted to shield her from the others. She could peruse the pages in relative privacy.

Flicking quickly, Harriet moved to the pages titled Macbeth. Just the usual names, some descriptions. Dark and dank. Pretty accurate for that cellar. Beautiful fields of purple heather. Also true. Sighing in frustration, Harriet turned the page over. The next one was titled Othello and didn't seem to contain anything that might help her. Idly flipping through the pages, Harriet saw plenty of Shakespeare's renowned plays. So much history in one little book. She felt almost guilty stealing it. Or she would, if it wasn't her only link to her home right now.

Nearing the end of the book, Harriet felt despair rise in her throat. It choked her like bile, burning its way across her chest and into her mouth. How could the old codger not have put anything in here to help?

Just as she was about to slam the cover shut in a fit of temper, a bold word caught her eye. Flicking the book back open, she studied it more carefully.

Turn it over three times. That was it. Nothing more.

Turn what over three times, Harriet thought crossly. But there was nothing else to explain the cryptic message, no other clues.

Slamming the book shut in annoyance, Harriet humphed. Then nearly cried out in despair as the old, weathered tome toppled from her grasp and flipped twice before landing in the dirt at her feet. Harriet quickly grabbed at it before Banquo or Fleance could see what she had, and she snagged the bottom of the book instead of the top. Turning it over so she could see the cover was intact, Harriet breathed a sigh of relief.

Then she stared in disbelief as a silvery light began to glow in the stables, lighting up the interior as it strengthened and doubled in size. Turn the book over three times, Harriet thought dumbly.

Chapter Seventeen

Harriet and Gideon had not seen the arrival of the three sisters in Birnam Wood. They had simply been there, in the clearing near the old oak tree when they had arrived, freezing and dishevelled. Watching them travel was entirely different.

The air shimmered with silver crystals, the light reflecting and bouncing around the gloomy stables. It was like watching a snowflake form, except the air felt warmer, not colder. As Harriet watched, mouth hanging open slackly, the silver mist took shape. The three sisters, as beautiful as ever, stood before her, their hands clasped together. Behind the stunning sisters, Harriet could see Banquo and Fleance's shocked faces. If the situation wasn't so serious, Harriet would have giggled at their expressions. Struck dumb was an understatement. Gideon, standing beside Harriet, hadn't moved an inch since the light had started to swirl. He was standing rigidly still, and Harriet could feel his disbelief from where she stood. She had to remember that the sisters had held him in thrall last time – she needed him to be sharp this time around.

"How did ye do that?" Banquo breathed, looking as though he didn't know whether he should cross himself or stare. He appeared to settle on the latter. His son followed suit.

The sister who first spoke to Harriet and Gideon in the woods when they arrived in Scotland was the spearhead of their triangle once again. She smiled luminously at Gideon, and the force of the expression stunned Harriet. God alone knew what it had done to Gideon, who had taken its full force.

"Ye have done well this night." The first sister drifted a little closer to Harriet and Gideon, her perfect face radiating light out into the darkness. "Ye have stopped some of the bloodshed, halted oor sister's path of destruction. Fer now. This one small change will have great bearing, though there is still much ter be done."

It seemed as though the fingers of evil couldn't touch them here, in the glorious bubble that surrounded the three sisters. As if sensing Harriet's thoughts, the sister inclined her head.

"Ye are safe, fer now," she confirmed. "Cailleach cannot touch yer for the moment."

With a rush of clarity, and a blinding pain in her head that made her want to cry out, Harriet saw it all. She remembered their first conversation, in the darkened woods their first night in Scotland.

We are in times of great turmoil. There are men – great men – who listen fer portents, rely on prophecies, but hear what they wish ter hear. We need you ter stop the bloodshed.

Harriet brushed the memory aside irritably. She knew that, but there was something else lurking just beyond her ability to grasp it, to fit it into the puzzle of their journey so far. With a last push into her mind, she had it.

We are sisters four. But our last sister has chosen a dark and dangerous road. Even more dangerous fer the one she controls. Cailleach, and Lady Macbeth.

You must find her, and stop her. Despite our power, we cannae. She is of our blood. If she succeeds, she will wipe out the power behind the throne of Scotland. All who come after will suffer. At the end of the solstice, after time moves into a new rotation around the sun, t'will be too late.

Harriet opened her eyes, not realising that she had closed them against the thoughts pummelling through her brain like a battering ram. She looked up, straight into the eyes of the first sister. Again, the sister nodded.

"Aye," she said heavily. "Despite our power, in this we are weak."

"What are your names?" Harriet asked. It seemed an odd question, given the many others that she could and probably should have asked, but being able to anchor at least that in her swirling thoughts might enable her to see more clearly.

"I am known as Samhain." Her voice was light, pretty. It matched her entire being. "My sisters are Lughnasadh and Imbolc. We are named for the duties that we have performed for many centuries." Samhain gestured with her hands as she introduced each of her sisters. She sighed heavily as she continued. "Our sister was named Beltane, after her sacred role in the turning of the seasons. But as the darkness crept into her, and her soul became blacker and colder, she took on the name of Cailleach. We hesitate ter say it usually, but we have protected this place where we stand for the time being and she cannae touch us. We aren't able ter hold it fer long, so we must decide what is to be done."

Harriet looked up at the sisters incredulously. Her hands spread wide, as if of their own accord. "If you can't stop her, what would you have me do?" Harriet's brow furrowed, her eyebrows raised sceptically.

"We cannae say," Lughnasadh said sadly. "We have tried fer centuries ter stop oor sister, ter bring her back ter us and stop the curse o' the Kings of Scotland."

"We're running out o' time," Samhain said, her voice urgent. "I can feel her – she is coming."

Samhain turned to Harriet. "Harriet, tis not about magic against magic, nor about changing oor sister. We fear that she is beyond even oor reach now. But ye have to try ter help contain the damage she is causing. Tis poisoning oor country." Samhain appealed to Harriet, her face now close enough for Harriet to see that her eyes were also a silvery-grey colour. They seemed mystical, as absorbing as Lady Macbeth's were. Which Harriet assumed was Cailleach's boiling, roiling malevolence hidden behind the mask of civility that Lady Macbeth allowed her to feign.

"Tis time ter call out oor Lords and men ter fight," Banquo said, his presence all but forgotten in the mesmerising company of the sisters.

"Hurry," Samhain urged. "She is coming. And she is riled."

Banquo hurried from the stables, and Harriet and Gideon moved with Fleance to look out from the doorway. Their view of the front gate of the castle was unimpeded. They were in prime position for the explosion that came moments later, almost at the same time as the bells pealed an alarm, a call to arms for the men of the castle.

Ladies came streaming through the castle doors, their screams echoing through the still night air. On their heels came unarmed men, racing for their weapons stashed around the keep of the castle and in their lodgings. Backing down the short staircase, their eyes fixed on something inside that only they could see, were the lords with their swords drawn. Horror flickered across their faces, revulsion in their eyes.

Harriet heard Samhain sigh behind her. She felt the rush of warmth as the three sisters surrounded her, gliding past on their way into the courtyard that was now well lit with flaming torches from within the Great Hall. Battling against the warmth was a blast of intense cold, streaming through the open doors of the castle proper. Framed in the doorway was Lady Macbeth – Cailleach: imposing, cold, impenetrable. Her face was a mask of icy glee as she watched the carnage that was reigning supreme ahead of her.

"My sisters," Cailleach said, raising her arms to the inky black sky. Her face was set, her eyes on the silvery women who were her kin. There was no familial warmth here – nothing left of the feeling between sisters. Harriet could sense resigned pain from the trio who stood together, resolutely, against their sibling gone mad. And she could sense power, and triumph, from the darkened soul disguised as Lady Macbeth who swaggered slowly down the staircase. She was assured of her win, Harriet had no doubt. Cailleach would settle for little less than total annihilation. With the castle locked to the outside world – the great gates resting silent and strong in their foundations – the people of Dunsinane were sitting ducks. Harriet felt like one too. She had absolutely no idea how to stop Cailleach. If her sisters had failed – for centuries, no less – what on earth could she do? Glancing up to the heavens for inspiration, a sign…anything, Harriet saw the blue star. It sat almost directly above its fainter mates, its crystal like beauty pulsing out into the blue-black darkness surrounding it. Like a stunning sapphire on a black velvet background, it winked high in the sky above the castle turrets.

Cailleach's malevolence crept across the ground towards Harriet, gliding along like the fog that had twirled around her ankles as she and Gideon had crossed the moors towards Birnam Wood. Her low chuckle slid over Harriet's skin, leaving goose bumps in its wake. The courtyard was eerily silent, despite the large number of people crowded into it. No one wanted to breathe, to make a sound, in case it attracted the attention of the Lady Macbeth who had clearly run mad. The castle inhabitants looked at their newly crowned Queen with undisguised horror. And given the sight of the Gruoch, no one could blame them.

Dressed as she was in unrelieved black, the lady looked like a glittering, mad raven. Her waterfall of long black hair was pinned up, exposing her slender neck that gleamed as white as the full moon that beamed down onto the assembled company. Jewels dripped from her throat and ears. Even her fingers glittered in the moonlight as she clasped her hands in front of her body, mirroring her sisters' stances. But, as always with Gruoch, it was the eyes that captivated. Harriet wasn't sure how much of those flashing orbs was the Lady Macbeth herself, and how much was Cailleach. Evil though she was, she was magnificent, standing on the bottom step with her head held high and her chin tilted imperiously. This wouldn't be an easy battle.

"Cailleach," Samhain moved steadily, shifting to stand slightly in front of her other siblings.

Cailleach sneered. "Always the protector," she hissed as she studied Samhain's serene face. Harriet glanced at it as well. Samhain seemed to be completely calm, and Harriet had no idea how. She had said herself that they were out of options and were relying on a young woman from another time and place who had inhabited their own for such a short period. What could she possibly have to offer that they didn't? They could prophesise and see the future. They had magical abilities, though Harriet wasn't sure exactly what they were capable of. She could sense it was no small gift, though. In comparison, Harriet knew she was plain, ordinary. Completely lacking in magical abilities whatsoever. There was no way that she would succeed where these sisters had failed. And it seemed she was out of time to try and think of a way out of this.

Cailleach snarled as her hands began to glow purple. Harriet saw Samhain hold out her own, bracing herself against the impact that was to come. In a flash, Cailleach launched what looked like an orb of purple fire at her sisters. It would have been a direct hit, except for Samhain's last minute deflection. People screamed, clawing and pushing instinctively away from the danger. Cailleach turned and took aim at the fleeing people, several of whom went flying through the air as the purple light tore through them. Their bodies slammed back to the ground, lying motionless in the dust. Harriet paled. The ground to the left of where the sisters stood was smoking, its surface blackened and scorched from the impact of Cailleach's power.

Cailleach let out a frustrated scream of pent up rage, and it screeched through the air like a flock of crows in flight.

"We cannae protect everyone," Imbolc murmured to Harriet. She stood closest to where they stood, partially sheltered by the doorway of the stables. "Even Samhain cannae extend her gift that far."

And that was something Cailleach obviously knew. She shifted closer to Samhain, but Samhain stood her ground. Harriet knew from her little trip to the cellars that Cailleach thrived on fear, on weakness. None of them could show any.

Ducking away from the spectacle in front of her, Harriet ran lightly to the other end of the stables. She could hear Gideon's hushed protest as she moved – he was as loathe to be separated from her as she was to leave him. But she needed to check. The sight that met her eyes made her smile. Banquo and Fleance had the small stone door ajar, and they were ushering lords, ladies, blacksmiths, traders, servants and peasants alike to relative safety beyond the castle keep. Excellent. That would significantly reduce the number of people Cailleach could harm.

Harriet raced back to her vantage point, in time to see Cailleach snarl and hurl another bolt of flame. Again Samhain deflected it, but it seemed to cost her. The magic was stronger than it looked from the outside, and it looked plenty powerful enough to the untrained eye. Behind Cailleach, on the steps to the castle, Macbeth and Lachlan had crept out of the main door, their gazes glued to the woman they thought was their wife and mother. Their eyes bulged wide in horror, their mouths slack as they watched the person they loved sneer and hiss, throwing fireballs of purple light around the castle keep. Most of it was aimed at the trio of sisters standing firm, supporting each other to stay strong against the onslaught. Some went wide, or were deliberately aimed to destroy the things that lay in Cailleach's path. Harriet could see from her face that she took vicious delight in obliterating the belongings others held dear. It seemed that Cailleach hadn't noticed the keep emptying of people, intent as she was on destroying those who stood in her way.

A grim smile full of intent spread across Cailleach's face, and her eyes flickered to the roof of the stables. Before her sisters could stop her, Cailleach sent flames streaming relentlessly into the thatch. It quickly caught alight in the dry, cool air of the evening.

"Ah," she said with satisfaction, surveying her handiwork as Gideon and Harriet crept out from the shadows of the stable doorway. It wouldn't be safe in there soon. The horses were already shifting restlessly in their stalls, smelling the smoke that was billowing upwards from the structure.

"I have an idea," Gideon murmured.

"I have to do something," Harriet cried in despair as she saw the renewed onslaught against the three sisters. They were flagging – they couldn't hold Cailleach off much longer. "Even if it just distracts her long enough to give them time to rest." Harriet squared her shoulders, threw her head back and walked out into the fray. Gideon grabbed uselessly at the air where her arm had been, horrified.

"Ach," Cailleach said, irritation creeping into her tone. "I thought I locked ye in the cellars. No matter." She changed the direction of her aim, the menacing glow of purple reflecting up into her obsidian eyes as she held it in her hand, ready to hurl at Harriet.

Harriet strode forwards, in front of the sisters, between Cailleach and the person she most wanted to live through this night.

"Stop," Harriet said in a commanding tone. Cailleach simply raised an eyebrow.

"Are yer going to halt me?" She taunted, raising her hand another inch. Her expression showed she was enjoying this, and Harriet doubted that there was much of the original Lady Macbeth left. She hadn't liked this woman from the start, but she felt genuine pity for the real Gruoch.

"I am," Harriet said firmly, surprising herself with the tone she managed to hit. "This is ridiculous. Why on earth would you be fighting against your own sisters?" Harriet's question made Cailleach pause, and something flickered in the depths of her soulless eyes.

"I would nae be, but they are between me and what I desire." Cailleach rolled her shoulders back, the fireball still nestled in her palm.

"And what is that?" Harriet asked, spreading her arms wide, her palms upturned. "What could killing us possibly give you?"

"Revenge," Cailleach hissed, her eyes darting around the keep. She frowned. There was hardly any audience left to watch her grand display of power. Harriet hurried to reclaim her attention.

"Revenge on who, exactly?"

"Tis not fer yer ter know," Cailleach snarled, advancing a step towards Harriet. Harriet didn't need to turn and look to know that the roof of the stable was catching, and would soon be well alight. Her heart ached for the animals inside, helpless to escape the impending inferno. But still, she focussed on what she was here to do.

"Let's see if I understand correctly." Harriet affected utter calm, her fingers steeped beneath her chin. It was a gesture she had seen her mother do often when one of her children was in trouble. "You are not Lady Macbeth. You are in fact Cailleach, the fourth sister of these three here." Harriet stumbled a little over the pronunciation of Cailleach's name – she didn't even attempt the others. "And you want revenge. On who and for what we don't quite understand, but perhaps a legend I heard earlier tonight might help. You see, there was once this girl," Harriet kept her gaze on Cailleach's face, not moving an inch. She saw the flicker in the depths of Lady Macbeth's glassy eyes and knew she had hit a nerve.

"This girl was in love, deeply in love, with a man who she understood was to be her husband." Harriet was exaggerating wildly from Banquo's story, but she didn't care. Something would hit home, and the wilder it was, the more likely it had some truth to it. After all, if anyone knew how stories could be twisted over time, it was her.

"It seems that the Kings of Scotland, and their wives, have suffered from...ill fortune, since around the time of Kenneth III." Harriet was repeating Banquo's fanciful legend bit by bit, putting her faith entirely in the stocky older man. She had no idea who any of these people were. Though she would wager Gideon would have an idea. And watching Cailleach's face as she was, she could see her words were making an impression. Harriet took a breath before she said the last of it.

"Legend says that her heart was broken when that man left her for another woman, the woman who would then become Queen of Scotland." Understanding dawned on Harriet, like tiny hammers driving the last of a masterpiece into place. Kenneth was the man. Cailleach was the broken hearted girl.

"How do ye know of that," Cailleach hissed, the purple ball in her hand pulsing with the rage that coursed through her veins. "How dare ye speak of it!" She lifted her hand and threw, and Harriet felt the burning trail whizz past her ear. Putting a hand to her head, she confirmed what her heart already knew. She was unharmed, thanks to the sisters standing at her back. For now. She needed to end this before anyone else was hurt.

"I know what it's like to have your heart broken, Cailleach," Harriet said, her eyes fixed on the woman standing opposite her. Her voice took on a lulling quality, almost without her will or effort. It just seemed to be there, ready for her to draw upon. Harriet took full advantage, using everything she had within her.

"But this is not the way. How many innocent people have to die before it's over? Before you feel avenged? The man who wronged you is dead, and has been for hundreds of years. The lady he married lays in the ground, cold and motionless, as she has for centuries. Who exactly are you hurting now?" Harriet could see she had Cailleach's attention, but her lip was still curled in a snarl and her face was a mask of frustrated fury.

"You deal in prophecies. Let me give you a truth. If you continue down this path, if you want this story to end the way you've started it, many will die. Banquo and Fleance have escaped tonight, but Gruoch will not. Lord Macbeth will not. He will die for taking the throne of Scotland, entranced though he was by you. His line will end, and a new line of kings will take their place. But if you don't leave them be, they too, will be decimated. Scotland itself will be decimated. Your culture will be stripped away. Your customs will be replaced by those of another country, and your right to rule your own people removed. That's what happens in the time that we come from, what has happened to countries in the recent past. If you keep tearing your country apart from within, it won't take much for someone outside to step in and claim it. You have to stop this, Cailleach," Harriet implored, her tone softening. "You were hurt, and it was wrong. But this is madness, and your entire country will suffer." Harriet could see from the expression infusing Cailleach's face that she knew Harriet was from another time, another place. She knew that Harriet had knowledge Cailleach couldn't possibly know, and Harriet could see it made her uneasy, unsure of herself.

Cailleach hesitated, her eyes flickering up to the stars, then back to Harriet as she stood before her, completely unarmed. Harriet held her flint black gaze, willing her to change her course.

Then she jumped out of her skin as Cailleach's face – Lady Macbeth's face – contorted. She screamed, an unearthly sound that echoed around the stone walls. The purple light that she had used as a deadly, violent weapon began to pour out of her, concentrating into a stream that wended its way past Harriet's shoulder to the trio of sisters beyond. As Harriet turned her incredulous face to Samhain, she saw the grim determination and grief etched onto her beautiful face. For that flickering moment, Samhain looked weary, and tired. Full of the grief that life visits upon everyone. She looked normal. Harriet could see where the original story of hag-like witches had gained its inspiration, with Samhain's glittering shield down. Not that any of the trio could ever look like a hag. It seemed Shakespeare's artistic licence was at play again. In Samhain's hands was a jewel of sorts, held within a twisted wire cage of Celtic knots. The stone within glowed with the violet essence that was Cailleach before the final stream of light shut off abruptly. Harriet whirled at the sound of Lady Macbeth collapsing to the ground. She lay still and motionless, her face unlike anything Harriet had seen in her time here. Gruoch looked calm. Tranquil. Her face was maternal, and lined with the passing of age. It was a beautiful, trusting face, and Harriet knew she was seeing the real Lady Macbeth for the first time.

With a cry, Imbolc and Lughnasadh glided to Gruoch's side. Samhain collapsed onto her knees, her knuckles white around the large locket of sorts that held her sister. Her face showed her grief, her frustration at failing her own sibling. It really couldn't have been helped. Imbolc ran her hands over the air clinging to Lady Macbeth's body. Lughnasadh bent her head and began to speak in Gaelic, her words tinkling on the night air until they were washed away by the next ones she uttered.

Lord Macbeth and Lachlan had taken the steps two at a time, and were ranged alongside Gruoch. Lachlan picked up his mother's hand and chafed it between his much larger ones.

"Come on Mama," he murmured, his eyes shadowed and haunted. Lord Macbeth looked like he was in physical pain, and probably shock too. Gideon had come to stand alongside Harriet as soon as he had been able to get past the sisters.

"I couldn't get to you," Gideon whispered, his voice anguished. "They held me back. It was as though I couldn't move my legs."

"That could have been Cailleach," Harriet murmured as they watched the sisters work to bring Lady Macbeth back. "That how she got me into the cellar again."

Samhain reached up to grasp Harriet's hand. Despite her weakness from the battle, Harriet could still feel the power that pulsed through the other woman's fingertips. She smiled as Harriet looked down at her, the same beatific smile she had gifted Gideon with earlier, though it looked a little more tired and weary. "You did it," she whispered.

"I didn't do anything," Harriet protested. Samhain gave a weak smile and let go of Harriet's hand. Gideon gave her his own to help her stand, then sat her down on a nearby mounting post. He grabbed at a pail hanging close by, intending to dunk it in the watering trough just metres away. The fire was starting to claim the roof of the stables – before too long it would be a proper blaze. And the horses were still inside. Harriet could hear them shifting, she could feel their panic as the heat closed in. Before Gideon could throw the water onto the burning thatch, the fire disappeared completely in a stream of silvery light. They both swivelled to stare at Samhain. She smiled faintly.

"'Tis all I have left." Then she slumped off her make-shift seat and fell to the ground.

Just as with a strangled gasp of air, Lady Macbeth woke up.

Chapter Eighteen

The wounded were tended in the great hall. Those who had been hit directly by Samhain's rage were healed by Imbolc and Lughnasadh as their sister lay in Harriet's bed, still unconscious. Harriet was assured she would wake soon – the magic that she had drawn upon that night had sapped all of her energy, and she would soon regroup.

Macbeth sat silently in his chair at the main table, watching with glassy eyes as his people were treated. He hadn't sat in the king's chair – hadn't been able to bring himself to do so since he had learned the extent of Cailleach's influence.

Macbeth had been horrified to learn that he had killed Duncan and his guards. He remembered nothing of it, and Harriet was inclined to believe him. A man couldn't fake an expression like that – one that conveyed bewilderment and disgust at the same time.

And a man who wanted the crown for himself didn't abdicate in favour of his own son.

Macbeth had sent riders to scout for Duncan's sons, Malcolm and Donalbain. They would claim what was rightfully theirs, and it would be handed over gladly by Macbeth and Lachlan. Lady Macbeth was still weak, but she was recovering and getting stronger by the hour. She did not remember Duncan's death either, but her blanked memory was even more extensive. Her last recollection was of being at Inverness Castle, departing for Dunsinane. After the first few miles of the trip, Lady Macbeth's memory faded to darkness. On hearing that, Harriet had exchanged a glance with Gideon. That would have been around the time that Lady Macbeth had been delayed behind her husband and Banquo, who were sitting at the crossroads, receiving a prophecy from the three sisters.

Harriet was anxious for Samhain to wake, because she knew in her gut that this sister held the key to their return home.

When the stars align, ye shall have ye reward. Those had been Samhain's words when they had first met in the woods.

The blue stars, Harriet thought with a jolt. Putting down the bandage she had been holding, Harriet hurried to the doors of the castle. It was well after midnight, perhaps in the early hours of the morning. The sun was yet to rise, and the pinpricks of light in the sky were still bright and sparkling. And there amongst the others, shining its shimmering blue light onto those around it, was her star. She knew it in her heart.

Gideon was at the bottom of the stairs, surveying the damage to the stable roof. He turned as he heard Harriet approach. He smiled at her, walking lightly up the steps to join her at the top.

"Gideon, I think I have the key," Harriet said excitedly.

"I thought we had to wait for Samhain to wake," Gideon frowned. He was even worse at attempting the traditional Scottish names than Harriet was. Harriet smiled and put her hand under his chin, tilting his face to look up the stars. The three blue points in the sky burned fiercely, and they were almost exactly aligned with each other. Gideon blew out a breath.

"We can't have much time," he said. "We need to get the book, and be ready when they do align." He had heard the words of the sisters as much as she had – and he knew far more about astronomy.

"This book?" A silvery figure emerged from the shadows behind them, coming out of the main doors of the castle. Samhain grimaced and held out the battered tome.

"Walking takes much longer, but I am not strong enough ter shift yet," she explained. Harriet took the book from her. She had nowhere to put it, dressed as she was with half a dress on under Gideon's cloak. As if she knew, Samhain waved a hand and Harriet felt her legs warm, shielded as they now were from the night air. They had been exposed in her improvised escape gown, but they weren't now that she was clothed in the dress and cloak Samhain had first given her. Samhain held Gideon's cloak out to him and he shrugged into it.

"Ye must go," Samhain said gently. "Tis time." She nodded to the stars overhead, confirming Harriet's theory was correct. Turning to Gideon, Samhain murmured, "Hold on tight to this one." Gideon nodded, looking at Harriet with solemn eyes.

Harriet didn't know if she had meant literally or figuratively, but considering it seemed to be her travelling power that moved them between realms, she took it literally. Tucking the book inside her cloak, Harriet grasped Gideon's hand.

A blinding flash in the sky above drew their eye, and Harriet sucked in a breath. Blue light seemed to rain down from the three points that became a pulsating trail of indigo fire. It was gorgeous. She smiled at Gideon as she felt the slight tug and pull on her body that she was getting more accustomed to recognising.

The next thing either of them felt was intense, breath stealing, numbing cold. Harriet sucked in air, only to fill her lungs with freezing cold water. She coughed and choked, searching frantically for the surface to ease the burning in her chest.

They broke through it at the same time, coughing and spluttering. Wiping the streaming water from her eyes, Harriet looked around to see her family, and Gideon's, staring at them both.

"You're not supposed to drink it, dummy," Mason taunted with a grin as he darted out of Harriet's reach.

They were back exactly where they had left, in the middle of the freezing Derwent River with their crazy families at the peak of the winter solstice. Harriet glanced up and searched the skies, finding what she was looking for in the first sweep of the glittering stars above. There they were, the three blue points. They no longer formed a line, with the top star, bright and pulsating, sitting slightly to the right of the others. It was over. For now, anyway.

As one, Harriet and Gideon struck out for the shore. The last days had been more than enough adventure, and it had certainly been a step up from the dip in the river they had been expecting.

On the frozen beach sat Carolyn. Alongside her, huddled in layers of beach towels and blankets, was Gideon's mother, Mary. The two had known each other for years – since their children had met in preschool, to be precise. It appeared to Harriet that they had been delighted to find each other to talk to while their crazy offspring and husbands ran amok in the freezing water.

"How did you end up going in, Harry?" Carolyn called, her face concerned as she took in her daughter's blue lips. She sprang up to layer her with towels, and Mary threw some at her son from her warm cocoon of blankets. Harriet could see her mother's teeth chattering – it was getting colder as the sun sank below the horizon.

"Well," Harriet said, rubbing at her soaked hair briskly with the towel. She was fully clothed in her own gear again, but there was no way she was taking any of it off out here. "You only get to do something like this once in a lifetime. Wouldn't want to waste it." With that, she walked off to the car, leaving Carolyn to stand with her hands on her hips, her mouth slightly open.

"Sometimes I don't understand that girl," she muttered as she snuggled back into the towel haven she had built with Mary.

"Harry!" Harriet turned as she heard her name shouted from the beach. She saw Gideon jogging up to her, a towel slung around his shoulders. He was fully clothed too, and he approached her uncertainly with his hands hanging awkwardly by his sides. He tried to shove his hands into his pockets, but they were too wet and he abandoned that effort quickly.

"So...," Gideon said, his words trailing off.

"So...," Harriet repeated, watching his face.

"What do we do now?" Gideon asked, his face perplexed.

"That would depend entirely on you, Lord White," Harriet said, smiling a little and turning away. She went around to the other side of the car, and she knew Gideon wouldn't follow her with her father's hawk eye on him from the water. They were all piling out now anyway, and their afternoon of revelry and chaos would soon be ending.

But, much to Harriet's relief, it seemed the chaos between her and Gideon was just starting.

Chapter Nineteen

The last of the red dye washed down the sink as Harriet squeezed the water from her hair. Weeks of washing had dulled the fiery colour down to a muted dark red – as close as Harriet could get to her natural light brown/auburn colour without a visit to the hairdresser.

Harriet heard her phone vibrate against the bathroom counter and she glanced at the display, smiling like a fool when she saw the name that popped up on it.

Lord White. No-one else knew who that was, and she wanted to keep it that way. What she had developing with Gideon was special, and she didn't need the likes of Gracie Finkle to destroy the tiny bud of feelings that were blossoming between them.

Harriet was sure that when she replied, Lady Hunter would pop up on Gideon's phone. They had been relatively inseparable since their return to their own time, and Gideon had joined Harriet in the quest for information about the time rifts and how they worked. The aged book was still hidden in Harriet's sock drawer…she felt guilty about taking it from the bookstore, but the more she thought about it, the more she knew in her gut that if she had wanted to, the old lady would have stopped her. Harriet was meant to have the tome.

The link between Harriet and Shakespeare – in a familial sense – was getting stronger by the day. With each generation that they traced backwards, they found more and more evidence that Harriet was indeed a descendent of the great poet.

The day they had discovered the direct Shakespearean tree around the time of the 14th century had been one of the happiest of Harriet's life. Right there, in amongst the other names recorded in the annals of time, was one that Harriet knew well.

Juliet. So they were related. Harriet knew that the connection she had felt with Juliet had been special – like a sister that she had never met. Harriet couldn't help but wonder if Juliet had the ability to travel through time rifts too – she'd just never used it.

"Harry!" Carolyn exclaimed as she walked past the bathroom door. She stopped to stare at her daughter. "Your hair! Why did you change it back?"

Harriet smiled. "I wanted to be me again," she responded, combing out her long tresses. Carolyn nabbed the washing basket and smiled.

"I'm glad to hear it," she said fondly, leaving Harriet to stare at her reflection in the mirror. Why would I have ever wanted to change who I am? Harriet thought, as she stared at the face she knew like the back of her hand.

Maybe it was getting older. Maybe it was the experience of travelling back with Gideon, or of knowing that she was related to one of the strongest, fiercest women she knew, but Harriet had found her confidence. She no longer cared what the Gracie Finkle's of the world thought (mostly), and she knew that she had friends who were constant and loyal, like Gideon. Losing old friends was uncomfortable and painful, but as Carolyn was want to say, sometimes you had to close a door to open a new one. Perhaps Tessa was the door Harriet had needed to close to open herself up to the possibility of new friendships.

And then there was Gideon. A month ago, Harriet would have told anyone who said she'd end up in a relationship with Gideon

White a flat out liar. But the Gideon she'd come to know during their time in Scotland was not the Gideon she thought she knew. Harriet liked this one much better.

As far as they could tell, the next alignment of the stars was six months away.

Harriet couldn't help but wonder, where would they send her next?

Explanatory Notes

Which characters are based on real people?

There has long been conjecture about which of Shakespeare's plays were based on real people, and to what extent. When creating a series like Into the Abyss, I've put my own spin on Shakespeare's characters and woven in elements of history that I have the benefit of knowing in the 21st century.

Characters such as Macbeth, Lady Macbeth (Gruoch), Duncan, Malcolm, Donalbain and even Lulach (Lachlan) are based on real characters from Scottish history. The historical events that sit behind *Macbeth* are different to what is portayed in Shakespeare's classic. For example, Duncan is defeated in battle by Macbeth, and contrary to the descriptions in the original, evidence suggests that Duncan was a much younger man, around the same age as Macbeth himself.

He was also an unpopular ruler, and Macbeth was well-received as the next King of Scotland. He ruled for nearly two decades, but came unstuck when he tried to pass power onto his son, Lulach.

Gruoch is a very interesting historical character. She has suffered the same fate as many famous and important women throughout history – the details that surround her are shadowy and murky. Which made it even more fun to play around with how to represent her! The granddaughter of Kenneth III, Gruoch Ingen Boite lived from around 1020 – 1054, her 34 years being fairly typical for the time she lived. Macbeth was indeed her second husband: Gruoch was married before 1032 to Gille Coemgáin mac Maíl Brigti, Mormaer of Moray. She had at least one son, Lulach mac Gille Coemgáin, later King of Scots (known in this story as Lachlan). Gruoch's first husband was killed in 1032, burned in a hall with 50 of his men.

Interestingly, two men are considered as likely candidates for the person who murdered Gruoch's first husband. Macbeth himself is widely considered the most likely to have killed his subordinate, then married his widow and taken on his son. This wasn't an unusual custom in the time these individuals lived, and we don't know what Macbeth's motivations were for marrying Gruoch. She might have been spoils of war, or perhaps Macbeth fell in love with her. In this tale, it isn't made clear what the reason was for their marriage, but it is clear that before Cailleach's possession of Lady Macbeth, they enjoyed a happy relationship with each other and Lulach. Lachlan (Lughlagh mac Gille Chomghain, in Modern Gaelic) is known in English simply as Lulach,. He was nicknamed "the Unfortunate", "the Simple-minded" and "the Foolish" and was King of Scots between 15 August 1057 and 17 March 1058 after his step-father (Macbeth) was killed. Following the Battle of Lumphanan, the king's followers placed Lulach on the throne. He has the distinction of being the first king of Scotland for whom there are coronation details available: and it was these details that inspired the coronation scene for Macbeth and Lady Macbeth. Lulach was crowned, probably on 8 September 1057 at Scone.

Lulach appears to have been a weak king, as his nicknames suggest. He was assassinated by Duncan's son, Malcolm III (Máel Coluim mac Donnchada), who usurped his throne and returned it to the previous family line.

Duncan was another character to appear in Macbeth who had his origins in the annals of history.

During the 10th century, there were dynastic conflicts in Scotland between two rival lines of royalty; one descended from Constantine I (reigned 862–877), the other from his brother Áed mac Cináeda (reigned 877–878). Historical sources claim that Kenneth II of Scotland (reigned 971–995) attempted to introduce new succession rules that keep the Scottish throne for his own descendants and exclude all other claimants.

While Constantine III of Scotland (reigned 995–997) did manage to rise to the throne, he was the last known descendant of Áed. With his death, the rivalry between descendants of Constantine and Áed switched to a rivalry between two new royal lines, both descended from Constantine.

One line hailed from Kenneth II and was represented in his son Malcolm II. The other line descended from Kenneth's brother Dub, and was represented by Kenneth III (rather confusingly!). According to the succession rules set by Kenneth II, Malcolm II was the legitimate heir to the throne of Scotland.

Malcolm II triumphed and passed the Kingship down to his own descendants.

However, the rivalry between the two lines survived the death of Kenneth III. In 1033, Malcolm II was still offing descendants of Kenneth III and Gruoch, another descendant of Kenneth III, was safely installed as the consort of Macbeth, King of Scotland. Interestingly, Macbeth's rival, Duncan I (the Duncan of our story) was the grandson and heir of Malcolm II. The bitter feud that had started a century before continued with them. Shakespeare twisted the characters, just as I have, to suit his literary purposes. The battle for supremacy and power was internalised within Macbeth, and he demonstrated the maelstrom and danger that represented ruling Scotland in this time.

Links between Scourge of Scotland and Macbeth

The Into the Abyss series was created as a way to bring Shakespeare to our next generations of readers. It isn't a recount, and as such, much of the rich tapestry that makes up

Macbeth found itself on the cutting room floor for this novel. Indeed, without such a process, these books would simply be a modernisation of a classic story, rather than an innovation.

Macduff appears very briefly in *Scourge of Scotland*, as opposed to his starring role in *Macbeth*. I sent him away to his castle in the north of Scotland to get him out of my way, quite frankly! I wanted the focus of this story to be on the ways in which characters are interpreted, and the biggest change in that respect is how the witches are seen.

In Shakespeare's original, the three witches are seen as hags – unattractive women who boil frogs legs under a full moon and have faces full of warts. In *Scourge of Scotland*, the witches are unearthly and beautiful. I mean, if you're a witch, wouldn't you get to choose your own appearance? Macbeth show the witches as a physical manifestation of their wickedness and malevolence, and in my version there's only one sister who displays those attributes. The difference in her appearance from those of her sisters is marked, yet she is still beautiful. This was a deliberate literary choice that was designed to show that evil isn't always readily recognisable. In fact, it can be tied up in a package as pretty as the most of pure of hearts.

Tanistry System of Inheritance and Laws of Transity

Rival branches of Scottish families fought for centuries for the right to the throne. Fierce fighting continued for generations as a direct result of the Tanistry system of inheritance, where the family would vote on who would be the next King from their extended branches. The King did not have the right to name his successor, although often he would try. This led to many bloody conflicts. The Tanistry system prevailed for quite some time and converted into the law of transity.

Sueno Stone

The Sueno Stone, a massive Pictish carved stone, appears in *Scourge of Scotland*, when the characters reach the apex of realisation about how Lady Macbeth came to be possessed by Cailleach. A local legend says that the Sueno Stone was where Macbeth originally met the three witches at a crossroads, and this is where the inspiration for this story arc came from.

Mysterious ancient stones similar to the Sueno Stone are dotted all over Scotland, but no other compares to the sheer size of the Sueno Stone.

Macbeth would certainly have been aware of the stone, which features a bloody battle scene on one side and a giant cross carved into the other.

Scone

Scone was associated with the traditions and rituals of Scottish kingship, and the time of Macbeth is a particularly interesting one. We are on the cusp of change in these centuries, with the influence of the French and Christian religion rising and the Pictish and pagan rituals of the past declining. Macbeth's coronation would almost certainly have featured some Pagan elements up on Moot Hill, with the coronation to be held in the Abbey that was found in 2007. Scourge of Scotland has the best of both worlds, combining the ancient tradition of the hill with the newly developing influence of the Church.

Stone of Scone/ Stone of Destiny/ Coronation Stone

Scone's famous inauguration stone, the Stone of Scone (also known as the Stone of Destiny or Coronation Stone), played a large role in the coronations of Scottish Kings. Future kings continued to be crowned there until 1651, with Charles II the last to go through the ancient ritual.

In 2007, archaeologists discovered the footprint of the medieval abbey. We can see where the high altar was, and where relics such as the Stone of Scone or Stone of Destiny were housed.

Cailleach

Cailleach ("old woman" or "hag" in modern Irish and Scottish Gaelic] comes from the Old Gaelic. In that language, Caillech meant "veiled one" – a particularly apt description for the Cailleach of this story.

Cailleach is associated with winter and wilderness, and alongside her sisters, is responsible for the changing of the seasons in

Scottish folklore. In Scotland she is also known as Beira, Queen of Winter. But she was someone entirely different before her love of Kenneth III twisted and warped her.

The legend in *Scourge of Scotland* says that Cailleach was a young girl in love with the King…the details of this legend remain sketchy, allowing the reader to draw their own conclusions about what might have transpired between Beltane and Kenneth III. In any event, she morphs into Cailleach, a spirit bent on revenge and blind to anything but her own jealousy.

Her sisters are named for the same phenomena: though in different ways. The reason that Samhain is the leader of the trio of sisters who remain pure is because in Scottish tradition, Samhain is the beginning of November. As a result, this spirit ushers in Winter. There are many parallels that can be made here, and some are from allusions to the many centuries that have passed since Cailleach was born. Responsible as she is for ushering in the winter months, or in metaphorical terms, her sister's wrath and rage, Samhain feels a certain sense of guilt and remorse. Her bravery in entrapping her own sister, and the grief she feels at doing so, are shown in the final battle scene between the siblings.

In the same pattern as Samhain, Imbolc is responsible for ushering in Spring and Lughnasadh the harvest time, or Autumn. Beltane, Cailleach's original form, was the keeper of Summer – the polar opposite of the spirit she became.

Scourge of Scotland is the second novel by young adult author, Marissa Price. It follows on from her authorial debut, *Vault of Verona.*

Loved the story?

Harriet's tale continues in *Into the Abyss: Angst of Athens*, coming to The Literature Factory publishing division in 2019!

www.ingramcontent.com/pod-product-compliance
Lightning Source LLC
Chambersburg PA
CBHW020941310726
48980CB00001B/6

* 9 7 8 0 6 4 8 1 2 7 9 5 6 *